SAM CRESCENT

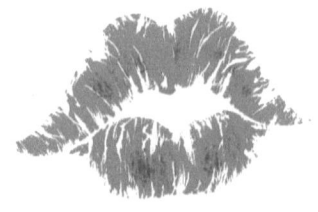

EVERNIGHT PUBLISHING ®

www.evernightpublishing.com

HIS TO TAKE

Copyright© 2018

Sam Crescent

Editor: Karyn White

Cover Artist: Jay Aheer

ISBN: 978-1-77339-654-5

ALL RIGHTS RESERVED

SAM CRESCENT

HIS TO TAKE

Sam Crescent

Copyright © 2018

Chapter One

"Are you ready for this?" Vincent asked.

"It's not every day you sell your soul, but I guess the Valenti family is worth it," Ronnie said.

Daniel Solano stared at his friends, who were both smirking at him. They thought it was funny that he was heading toward the home of the woman he'd been contracted to marry. He didn't even want to marry, but according to his father, at thirty years old, it was his duty to marry and start producing heirs. He thought it was a load of bullshit, but then at thirty his father had married his mother.

The men were allowed time to sow their wild oats, and to get all the fucking out of their system. Most of the men had a mistress, and that was more than fine. Running the mafia was a dangerous business. Wives and children were meant to be protected while mistresses were always collateral.

"Who are you supposed to be marrying again?" Ronnie asked. He held the file on the Valenti family. Daniel imagined all families had files on each other. It was a way of keeping track of everyone, and also finding any loose ends that might need cleaning up.

"Louisa."

"Ah, the one that loves to shop," Vincent said.

Daniel had seen plenty of pictures of his future wife. She didn't exactly thrill him, not in the least. In fact, she looked as shallow as any woman could be.

"She's awful for the pocket, but she'll do fine to look the part," he said. He had no interest in her. In fact, her pictures didn't even inspire a hard-on. She wasn't his type. Everything about her screamed fake, and he was done with fake. In their world, fake got you killed, but then, so did being real.

Rubbing at his temple, he finished getting dressed while his friends continued to read out all of the problems with the Valenti family. If they weren't one of the wealthiest and deadliest families in the world, he wouldn't be having to go to this damn Thanksgiving dinner. As it was, his father didn't give him much of a choice, and seeing as the Solanos didn't have any daughters, they couldn't make a match with the Valenti sons.

Louisa was the oldest daughter but not the oldest child.

The drive over to the house wasn't exactly appealing to him. His father was going over and over about his duty and how he'd had his time to play the reckless boy, but that stopped now.

Daniel didn't see what the problem was. He'd not sired any bastards while he'd been "playing around" as his father called it.

Alfie Valenti, along with his wife, were there to greet them. It wasn't always customary to have Thanksgiving with other families, but, seeing as this weekend would also be the engagement announcement, plans had changed.

Climbing out of the car, Daniel shook Alfie's hand, and then his wife's. Out of the corner of his eye, he saw Louisa in the house. She was leaning up against one of the soldiers, running her hands over his chest.

Well, that would have to stop. He wouldn't run the risk of having any heir that wouldn't belong to him.

Daniel had been aware of her affair with one of her guards and was surprised that her father hadn't put an end to that some time ago.

"It's good for you to be here, Frank," Alfie said, looking at Daniel's father. The two older men embraced.

Once they were inside, Louisa looked on her best behavior, but he saw through the façade, and he wasn't happy.

"Daniel, I'd like you to meet my daughter, Louisa," Alfie said.

"It's nice to finally meet the man I'm supposed to be marrying," Louisa said.

Her mother cursed her and warned her to be quiet.

He took her hand, giving it a polite shake. "Charmed."

Louisa gave him a dazzling smile. Daniel couldn't help but look toward the guard she was screwing. The look wasn't lost on Louisa, and her smile slipped a little bit.

He was no fool, and there was no way he'd ever allow anyone to treat him like one.

"Something smells delicious," he said, looking toward Mrs. Valenti, who beamed at him.

"That would be Mary. She's cooking Natalie's favorite."

Daniel looked toward Alfie, who chuckled. "My youngest daughter. She's due to arrive any second now. It's just like her to be a little late. I swear, she'll be late to her own funeral."

"You shouldn't let her leave by herself," his wife said.

A look passed between the couple and she let it go, stepping away.

Louisa laughed, taking his arm. "Don't mind them. They're always arguing about Natalie."

He had information on Natalie. She was the youngest daughter to Alfie Valenti, and the one that also seemed to be the most mysterious.

"She's not here?"

"She will be. Dad tends to let her roam free, and seeing as there's no war now, it's not like he has to keep her indoors, so he likes to give her some freedom." They entered the kitchen. "Mary, I'd like you to meet Daniel Solano. My fiancé."

He saw a large woman with ruby red cheeks and a pleasant smile. "Hello, Miss Louisa."

Mary shook his hand.

"Dinner smells delicious."

"Thank you, sir. Any sign of Natalie?" Mary asked, turning her attention to Louisa.

"Not yet."

"Blast. I should have known not to trust that girl to stop by and get me butter," Mary said.

Daniel frowned as he watched Mary head back to the stove and begin muttering something about butter being the key to a happy life.

"My sister spent a lot of time with Mary growing up. Mom didn't want much to do with her. So, our wedding, I was thinking we could go with a traditional white, but I'd love gold. I want gold leaf available as well." She began to prattle on about the wedding, and he wasn't really listening to her.

Looking around him, Daniel felt … rage. A

burning rage that he was marrying this false little bitch, and that he was about to put his name to her, and not only that, he'd have to stick his dick inside her. Just the thought was repellent. He'd do his duty though. It's all he ever really knew.

He knew what the family name required of him. His training to take over from his father had started when he was just a boy. When you were in the mafia, you didn't get the chance to have a childhood. The girls that were born rarely got one either. They were used as pawns in all of the old men's games.

Daniel watched the guard he'd seen Louisa with, and knew the bastard wanted to hurt him right now for even touching her or being near her. That soldier needed to learn his place. He was about to pull Louisa into his arms and give the man a real show when the sound of the door slamming open made him go for his gun.

"I'm so sorry I'm so late," a woman said, shouting to be heard. "It's so cold out there. I'm surprised I didn't freeze to death." She then made a noise, and he looked toward Louisa, who rolled her eyes.

"I sometimes wonder if she does that to annoy Mother."

Glancing past her shoulder, he saw the warmth in Mary's face as the woman in question entered the kitchen.

"You're late!" Mary said, suddenly looking stern.

"I know. I know, Mommy." The woman moved up to Mary and hugged her tight. "I got you goodies though."

He figured this woman was Natalie, and then he really looked at her. Louisa and all the women he'd seen in the household were dressed to impress. Expensive evening gowns, makeup so thick it was impossible to really see their faces, and their hair didn't look out of place at all.

This woman though, wore a pair of jeans and a large black and white checkered top. Her brown hair was bound at her neck in a loop, with several strands falling out. She looked like she'd just gotten out of bed, apart from how bright her gaze was. Her eyes twinkled as she looked at Mary.

"It's time you showed up," Louisa said, drawing the woman's gaze.

Finally, the woman looked up.

Daniel wasn't sure what happened to him, but the moment her eyes were on him, something fucking changed. Everything seemed to freeze up, and he couldn't look anywhere else but at her. He'd never been a lover of curves, but just looking at her, his mouth watered. She was all rounded hips, big tits, and full thighs that a man wanted to get lost in. She was on the plumper side, much bigger than Louisa, but that didn't make her any less sexy. In fact, Daniel couldn't recall seeing a sexier woman.

"I was getting stuff, Louisa. Wow, have you decided to be like Mom now?" Natalie asked.

At the mention of Mom, the sparkle died just a little. Not only that, Mary was fussing around her, and she'd called the cook "Mommy."

He was so fucking confused.

Louisa grabbed his arm. "Natalie, honey, I want you to meet my fiancé, Daniel Solano."

Natalie looked between them, and she smiled. He had a feeling there was not a lot of love between the two sisters.

****

If Natalie could have gotten out of coming home for Thanksgiving, she would have. In fact, she'd planned to be very busy, and was about to find a job when Mary called her and begged her to come. The moment Mary begged, she came running. Out of everyone in the Valenti household, apart from her father, Mary was the only person who liked her.

Her father had called her and told her about the impending engagement that would be announced.

She wasn't an idiot. Her family was part of the mafia, so she had no doubt that somewhere along the way this was a contract that was made in the dead of night to help bring peace.

Not that she had a problem with peace.

Natalie hated to be part of the mafia. The less she had to do with the family, the better. She'd even gone so far as to strike a deal with her father so she'd never be dragged into this life. From a young age, she'd been next to Mary in the kitchen. She knew more about serving the family than being part of it.

Looking at Louisa's dress, then down at her own attire, she saw the difference there. Still, she'd sit at the table like her father would demand, and have to deal with their ridicule. Even her brothers would join in, and that was going to be embarrassing.

"Hello," she said, smiling at the man destined to be Louisa's husband. In her thoughts she wished him good luck, but that was pretty much it.

He stepped forward and held his hand out for her to take. She rarely touched anyone else, and her father always warned her about accepting handshakes.

Her father was simply paranoid.

Stepping around the counter, she placed her hand within his, and was shocked by how small her hand looked in comparison to his. She took a deep breath and offered him a smile.

"Congratulations on your impending marriage. I'm sure you'll have many happy years together."

He didn't say anything.

Out of the corner of her eye, she saw Ben was having a hard time controlling his expressions. He looked ready to murder the man.

Alfie Valenti chose that moment to enter the kitchen, and all negativity left her as he pulled her into his arms and hugged her tight. Where her mother couldn't stand her, and had even tried to kill her, her father adored her. She knew that she'd become a constant problem between her parents. Even though her mother tried to kill her, there was no way her father could punish her without their being repercussions, as her mother came from a powerful family too. It became an internal family problem, one her father always tried to deal with, but it didn't matter. Natalie avoided her mother all the time and did everything to take care of herself.

She'd spent a lot more time around him than any of her other siblings had, which angered them. It's not like he had a choice though. When he caught his wife ignoring her in the bath as a baby, then another incident, Alfie had given her to Mary, and in doing so, he'd kept an eye on her.

"I'm so sorry I'm late," she said.

"Nonsense. Better late than never."

Over his shoulder, she caught sight of her mother glaring at her, and she didn't say a word.

"Ah, Daniel, this is my youngest daughter here," Alfie said.

"We've been introduced. It's a pleasure, Natalie."

The way he said her name confused her. She looked toward Louisa, who normally liked to take a moment to tease her, but her gaze was on Ben. Wow, this was like a nightmare waiting to happen, and why she normally avoided everything.

"How long until dinner?" Alfie asked.

"Another hour, sir."

"Good, good. We're going to take drinks in the living room," Alfie said.

"I'll bring them out." Natalie spoke up, wanting to avoid being in the room for too long.

"You're not the servant here," Alfie said.

"I like bringing drinks. You know that."

He shook his head, and she watched each of them go. When she was sure no one could hear her, she stepped up to Ben. "You need to get your head together."

Ben glared at her. "I don't have to take orders from a baby."

"I'd listen to her, young man," Mary said. "They catch wind of what's going on between you and Louisa, and you're dead. Just another in a long line of Louisa's lovers."

Natalie stared at him. He had that "boy next door" look, but he didn't interest her. Ben never had. "You're not the first guy she's taken under her wing, and given the little victim speech, Ben. She'll get you killed when she bores of you."

"She loves me."

"I'm sure she does, but even so, be careful." Natalie stepped away and made her way toward the drinks, and began to pour.

Mary moved up behind her, taking her shoulders. "Don't cry, my sweet."

"They hate me. Why did I have to come here?"

"The Solanos are powerful men, Natalie. I'm sure your father will deal with what they need, and then you can go back to living your life."

She glanced down at her attire and sighed. Her life was … complicated.

At the tender age of ten, she'd already figured out what her father did, what the name Valenti meant, and she'd gone out of her way to break away from the family that didn't want her. Apart from her father, everyone else hated her.

She often wondered if she was adopted, or if she was really her father's mistress's baby. It didn't really matter at all. Baby or not. Her mother couldn't stand her, and no one was about to tell her the truth.

"I'm sorry I was late."

"I'm getting used to it." Mary kissed her cheek, and Natalie collected the last of the glasses. Once outside the door to the main sitting room, she looked at the guard there, Phillip. He had a young wife and three beautiful children.

"You want to go in there?" he asked.

She shook her head. "I want to leave."

He chuckled. "You'll do fine."

"And then cry near the pool later on; I know the drill."

"You've got more strength than you realize."

"I've been told kindness is a weakness."

"It's not. Don't let anyone else get you down." He did something no soldier was supposed to do, and patted her arm.

She took another deep breath. "Wish me luck."

"Break a leg."

Natalie smiled, biting her lip to contain her laughter. She didn't like that show of support. Break a leg? It made no sense. Why would she even want to break a leg, or something like that?

Shaking her head, she entered the room, and all gazes turned toward her.

"I come bearing offerings from the kitchen," Natalie said.

Words rarely failed her, but she found a big smile, and a chatty girl tended to make a lot of people leave her alone.

She put the tray on the table and took the scotch toward her father. It was the expensive sort, and he only ever liked it for family gatherings.

He took the glass and pulled her in for a hug. "How are you doing?"

Natalie turned to face the room. Her brothers and sister were all glaring at her. Their father was always openly affectionate with her, and it always drove them crazy. They'd been taught to be seen and not heard.

"I'm doing good. I've applied for three colleges so far, and I'm hoping to hear back any day now."

She'd taken a gap year from high school, and then another year as she had to start applying for scholarships. In this room, people knew her as Natalie Valenti, daughter to one of the most powerful men in the country.

To the outside world, she was Natalie Carmichael, struggling student, with no one. This was the price she had to pay in order to get out from being part of the family. Even now, at twenty years old, she could see the disappointment on his face when she'd begged him four years ago for a free life. A life away from being a man's wife, and a tool. She'd used his love against him.

It was the only time she'd been mean.

"If you loved me, Dad, you'd let me do this."

Against all the odds, he'd agreed. She couldn't have the Valenti money. Her way had to be made without any help from him. She'd live with Mary, and he'd have a guard, just in case. For the most part, Natalie Valenti ceased to exist as she'd never been in the public eye, but that didn't mean there wasn't a paper trail. She was aware of the risk that she took every single day to be her own person. Her father had promised that only people who did some serious digging would find her. To the outside world, she was Mary's daughter, but there was only so much that he could do.

Their agreement was still a sore subject with him though.

"You'll get in," he said.

She smiled up at him. "You must be proud."

Taking her glass, she lifted it in the air. "To Louisa and Daniel, on your engagement."

"It's not final yet," he said.

She turned her gaze to Daniel. From the moment she'd entered the room, he hadn't taken his eyes away from her, and she kept trying to ignore it.

"Yes, let's not get ahead of ourselves," Alfie said. "To peace, to the Solanos, and to the Valentis. Let's hope we can make an agreement that is mutually satisfactory."

She saw the humor in Daniel's eyes, and she didn't like it.

Chapter Two

"You're staring at the youngest daughter," Vincent said. "And I mean creepily a lot."

Daniel took a deep drag on his cigarette. He rarely smoked, but he used it as a tool to get away from situations. "Anyone else find anything strange about her?"

"You mean the way she's dressed?" Ronnie asked.

"Not just that. The way she is with everyone."

"She's Alfie's favorite, no denying that. You can see it, even if he does try to hide it. If her brothers and sister could have killed her with a single look, she'd be long dead," Vincent said.

He dropped the cigarette to the ground and stubbed it out with his toe.

"What do we know about her?" Daniel asked. He couldn't get rid of this intrigue with her. That one look and he needed to know more.

"You've seen the file," Ronnie said. "There's not a lot on Natalie Valenti."

"I want to know why."

"I can make a few calls," Vincent said.

"Do it."

His friends nodded and began to make the call as Daniel headed back to the house.

He stepped inside and was rounding the door when someone crashed against his chest. She fell back, and he quickly reached for her hand, holding her close so that she didn't fall and bang her head.

"I'm so sorry. You appeared out of nowhere, and I'm not usually such a klutz."

He stared down into the brown gaze of Natalie. Her eyes were so expressive. He wondered if she even realized how much.

Quickly she pulled away from him. "I'm so sorry."

"You've got nothing to be sorry about." He offered her a smile.

Her hands were clenched at her sides, and he wanted to know everything about her. Why was she here? What did she do? How did she fit in with the rest of her family?

"Hurry up," her mother said, capturing her arm and pulling her into the rom.

Daniel watched as Natalie gasped. The pain was clear on her face, and without thinking, he reached out to where her mother touched her arm.

Everything froze as she looked at him, alarmed.

"Let her go. I'll take her inside."

The moment her mother let go, Natalie covered the spot, rubbing her arm. She clearly didn't like showing pain, and he didn't press.

Now was not the time or the place to be causing a scene. "Shall we?" he asked.

She nodded, taking his arm and smiling as they made their way into the room. "Thank you."

He'd already swapped Louisa's place setting with Natalie's before he headed out for a smoke.

"Oh, look, we're sitting in the same spot."

They were near the center of the table, away from all parents. Of course, this was supposed to be for Louisa and him to get close, but he had no interest in that.

Holding out her chair, she stared at the table, then at him. "Ladies first?"

"She's not a lady."

He heard someone mutter the words and wondered if she did. Natalie gave no sign that she had, sitting down. Her cheeks however, were a shade redder, and he knew she'd heard it.

"That's not where you're supposed to be sitting," her mother said.

"It is," Daniel said, speaking up.

All gazes fell on them.

"That's Louisa's seat."

"Someone made a mistake then," he said, staring at the woman who clearly hated Natalie.

"I'll just move."

He put a hand on her shoulder. "Your name is there, and you're going to sit there."

"Everything is settled," Alfie said. "There's no problem with her sitting there."

After another few seconds of arguing, Natalie stayed there, and he smiled at everyone. Daniel was used to getting his own way.

"You moved the card names, didn't you?" Natalie asked.

"I don't know what you mean."

"Mom always does the cards and where people sit. It's the one area of control she likes to take."

"Yeah, well, I'm supposed to be married to Louisa for the next fifty years, so I'm sure I can sacrifice another day."

Natalie glanced toward Louisa. "You saved me, to be honest. My brothers would have made my life a misery."

"Yeah, I had noticed there's not a lot of love lost there."

She shrugged. "Bad childhoods, I guess."

He stared at her and waited to learn more.

The first course in the Thanksgiving dinner came out.

Natalie was the only one to say thank you for her meal, and Daniel did the same. He couldn't take his eyes off her.

She enchanted him. There was no other word for it.

"Are you looking forward to your marriage?" she asked.

"Nope. This is not a marriage that I ever want to take part in but more a duty."

"That's … sad."

"Do you believe marriage should be for love?" he asked, wanting to know her thoughts.

"I think marriage for normal people in the normal world should be for love. I'm not an idiot. I'm aware that in this life, marriage tends to be more of a business contract."

"Or an agreement to keep the peace. It's harder to start a war when half of your family would be on the hit list."

She nodded her head. "Exactly. It's not pleasant, is it?"

"You don't have a problem with what your family does?"

"It's not that I don't have a problem with it. I just learned a long time ago that if they want to do something, they'll do it regardless of if someone wants you to or not. I can't help who I was born to."

Once again, he glanced down at her attire. She wasn't wearing any fancy gowns or anything like that.

"You're not dressed like a Valenti."

She smiled, and that completely blew him away. "I'm not really a Valenti. You'll not see me dressing like one."

"Now why would that be?"

"It's top secret. I'd have to kill you if you ever found out."

He leaned in close, and she didn't pull away from

him. "I like to live on the edge. I'm sure I could survive."

"Ah, but you see, Mr. Solano, I'm not."

"Daniel. My name's Daniel."

She smiled at him again. "Then call me Natalie."

Again, he leaned in close so his lips were near her ear. "I intended to."

She pulled back, and someone cleared their throat.

"How are the days of scrubbing?" Louisa asked.

Daniel watched as Natalie's cheeks heated.

"I mean, you were working as a cleaner at one of Dad's offices, right? What is it now? Are you being hired out?"

Daniel's hands clenched into fists. He didn't know what the fuck was going on, but the insult she'd just dealt out to Natalie would not go unpunished.

His cell phone vibrated, and Natalie spoke up.

"I'm actually working at a diner. I waitress five days a week, and I do part time in the library. I'm able to get all the studying in to be ready for college."

"I'm going to say it. You're more of the intellectual type. Not wife material, or anything else," one of her brothers said.

Daniel couldn't believe what the fuckers were saying.

Vincent: **Natalie Valenti is also Carmichael. She's not part of the family anymore.**

That didn't make any sense, but he didn't have time to put anything into words.

"You don't need to be a wife to enjoy life, Anton, you should know that," Natalie said.

"How is the life outside treating you?" the other brother asked.

"Enough," Alfie Valenti said.

All heads turned to him, and thunderous rage

covered his expression. He looked ready to kill all of them, and Daniel had a lot more respect for him.

"This is a family dinner."

"Then she shouldn't be here," his wife said. "She's not family, remember?"

"I can just go and eat—" Natalie went to stand, grabbing her plate.

"Sit your ass down," Alfie said, getting to his feet. He slammed the palm of his hand against the table. "She's a Valenti, and this is a private moment. She will be part of it."

His wife looked ready to say something else.

"Say one word, wife, and believe me, you'll regret it."

Daniel glanced over at his parents, who had been watching the interaction. This was not normally something two families would ever share. The discontent was clear, and Natalie looked miserable.

Conversation struck up again, and he didn't like how withdrawn she was. No matter what he tried to say to her, she just smiled, and offered him polite, one-word replies, which only served to piss him off. He didn't want that. He wanted to know what she was thinking, feeling, and to find out what the fuck had just happened.

****

After helping with the dishes, Natalie stepped out into the garden. She didn't bother with a jacket or anything. The fresh air helped to numb all of her thoughts. Most of the time she was home, she ate in the kitchen unless her father demanded her presence at the table. Today had been … horrible.

She'd not been able to eat much. Her brothers had taken a few more jabs at her weight, her appearance, and everything that always made her feel less of a woman. She liked the way she was. Her curves were part of her, and she had no intention of changing that just to please her mother, not that it would matter regardless. Her mother would just find another excuse to not like her.

Pushing her sweater down over her stomach, she moved toward the pool and took a seat in one of the chairs.

She loved the garden. Eric, the man who maintained it, would often let her help him weed out the flower beds, or plant new seeds. He'd often tell her that she was a hardy plant. One that was beautiful, but only ever really seen when you chopped down all the other flowers.

A lot of the staff at the house were aware of the family's hatred of her.

"Should you be all alone?" Daniel asked, surprising her.

He lurked in the shadows, and she thought he'd be having after dinner drinks or something, at least spending some time with Louisa.

"I just wanted some fresh air."

Daniel nodded, taking a seat opposite her.

"I'm sorry about dinner," she said.

"It's fine. That was not your fault. Does this have anything to do with sibling rivalry or something like that?"

She shook her head, chuckling. "No. Nothing like that."

"Your brothers and sister hate you."

"I know. My mother's not a huge fan either."

"Why is that?"

She opened her mouth to respond and then closed it again. Her life as a Valenti warned her off revealing everything. Biting her lip, she stared at him. "It's nothing."

"I just sat at dinner, and I'm going to be family. It

doesn't take a rocket scientist to know something is going on there."

She sighed. "Not a lot is going on."

"You work. You don't wear expensive clothes. Your mother looks ready to hurt you."

"Kill me, more like," she said, laughing.

But the laughter sounded false to her own ears. She didn't know why, only that overwhelming sadness filled her. "My brothers and sister hate me because my dad likes me." She shrugged. "Not a lot I can do about that." She sighed. "Mom … I don't know. Maybe she just snapped or something. I'm not really sure of her reason, I only know that she has a reason to hate me." She ran fingers through her hair. "When I was little, I don't really remember a whole lot. I only know what I heard in whispers. Mom was supposed to take me for a bath. Babies can drown, or something like that. Mom watched as I lay in the bath, and she kept filling the tub. Dad barged in as my head was submerged. There was another incident where she tried to smother me with a pillow. This has something to do with after giving birth, I think. Postpartum depression, maybe? I don't know. Either way, Mom has never liked me."

"That's her loss."

"Then we move on to my brothers and sister. Now, I think that's because Dad was around a lot more. He didn't really have a choice. On two occasions that I know of, Mom tried to kill me. I think for anyone that's a little … crazy. He spent a lot more time with me whereas my brothers and sister didn't get all that much time."

"So, jealousy?"

"Yeah, I guess." She shrugged. "Either way, I don't really fit into the Valenti life." And it was why she was willing to work hard not to be part of it. No matter what she did, they always found a reason to hate her.

From doing too well at school, they'd accused her of being an overachiever. When she put weight on, her mother would make her life hell, buying clothes that were too small and making her wear them, mocking her. All of this was done behind Dad's back.

She was surprised she hadn't snapped before now.

Oh, well, she couldn't do anything about it.

This was her life at the moment. One day, she may stop coming home. She'd thought about cutting and running a long time ago. She lived her own life for the most part, except for the guard that her father had on her. The man tried to pretend he was just a friendly neighbor, but she knew differently. Her father kept a watch on her at all times.

Running away was so tempting.

"What about Carmichael?" he asked.

This made her pause as she looked at him. "What do you know about Carmichael?"

"That you're Natalie Carmichael."

Her heart began to pound, and she didn't like that. "Are you looking forward to being married to my sister?"

"Nope. She holds no interest for me."

"Maybe you should go inside. Talk to her a little."

"All that woman wants to do is shop, talk about gossip, and screw her guard."

This now made her gasp, and she looked toward the house. Ben was a nice guy. Sure, once he started screwing Louisa he'd been an ass to Natalie, but before then, he was nice.

"You knew?"

"It's not hard to see. I'm not blind, Natalie. I'm guessing he's not the first one either."

She didn't say anything. What was the point? If

he knew about Ben, then he knew about others.

Running fingers through her hair, she stood up. "I have to go."

Daniel caught her wrist and pulled her back to the chair. She didn't like how easily he got his own way. It didn't impress her, and it never would.

"You can't keep pushing me around." She wrapped her arms around herself and rubbed her hands up and down her arms.

He removed his jacket, placing it across her shoulders. "I can do what I want. I could kill you right now and no one would know it was me."

She glared at him. "Then do it."

"You're asking me to kill you?"

"I'd like to see you try."

Daniel smiled. "You're an interesting woman, Natalie."

She shook her head. "I'm not interesting. I'm really boring, actually."

He tilted his head to the side. "You and I have different views on what we consider boring."

She didn't say anything.

"Will you be married off to one of the men in this game? A peace toy?"

Natalie shook her head. "No."

"Why not?"

"You ask a lot of questions."

"I figured I knew everything about the Valentis. Then you walked into the kitchen today. The spite your family has for you. Not to mention how you stick out like a sore thumb. It's all very confusing. I'm wondering if I should call off the wedding."

She knew this wedding was important. Her father had been planning it for a long time. Peace between the families was necessary.

"I'm ... I made a deal," she said.

He tilted his head to the side again, and she knew he was handsome. He had a scar down one side of his face, but that didn't detract from his sexiness. The scar made him look deadly, sinister. He was the man in charge, and could do whatever the hell he wanted, and no one had a choice but to fall in with his demands. It was kind of scary.

"You made what kind of deal?"

"I knew what my family did. I knew I didn't want to be part of that, so I struck a deal. I hold the Valenti name within these walls, but outside I'm a Carmichael. I make my own way. I work. I work a lot, and I don't have to be put on the marriage chopping block. I gave up the name, the money, and the luxury."

She also gave up the loveless marriage, and everything else. She shouldn't be coming home at all, but her dad liked to see her as often as he could. Thanksgiving and Christmas were two occasions he wouldn't allow her to stay away.

They agreed he could visit her for her birthday, but that was it.

So far, everything had worked out perfectly. "Don't ... ruin this marriage. I know it means a lot to him."

Daniel looked at her. "You don't want to get married?"

She smiled. "Someday I do. I'd love to be married, and have a couple of kids, but I don't want this kind of wedding. Something that has been written down on some paper with the knowledge that it would bring two families together." She shrugged. "I guess I just want to be a normal person. Didn't you want to be that before you became this?"

He shook his head. "All I've ever known is the

Solano way. I will take over, and the blood will be on my hands."

She shivered.

He gripped the lapels of the jacket and closed it around her. "We should get inside. I don't want to be accused of killing you."

She chuckled. "There's a long list of people trying."

He shook his head. "That's not funny."

"What you need to do is find the funny in it."

Chapter Three

A few days later Daniel sat in Alfie's office. Alfie's sons and closest family were there, all men of course. Daniel's own family was there, along with Vincent and Ronnie. He tapped his fingers on the arm of his chair as he listened to the details of the upcoming marriage. The binding contract, what would become his by joining their two families together.

In the back of his mind, he couldn't get Natalie out of his head. This weekend, he'd found every single opportunity to be with her. He found her smile refreshing. Her wit left a lot to be desired, but she was funny. She made him laugh, and there wasn't any falseness to her. Fashion or gossip were the last things she ever talked about.

She also tried to constantly sing Louisa's praises, and he noticed she kept him away from Ben, the soldier screwing Louisa.

Not only had he been watching Natalie though, he saw the soldiers were all nice to her. No one had a bad word to say about her, and for him, that meant something. She didn't flirt, tease, or tantalize them. Whereas he'd watched Louisa, and she showed off her body in a way that was taunting them. They couldn't have her.

Natalie stirred him.

Louisa left him cold.

There was no way in hell that he was going to marry that bitch.

"No," Daniel said, drawing all the men's gazes to him.

"Excuse me," Alfie said.

"I'm not marrying Louisa Valenti."

There was silence, and then chaos as both men

faced off with each other.

Daniel saw the impending war if he didn't marry the Valenti girl, but he couldn't put his name to such a woman. Natalie, however, she was another thing.

"I want Natalie," he said, speaking up.

Both of his friends were staring at him. They had seen his interest and they'd even spoke about it, but they told him it was useless to want someone who would never want him.

He didn't care.

Natalie was his. Every time he was with her, he felt her inside him, and there was no way in hell that he was going to ever let that go.

"Natalie's not on offer," Alfie said.

"This is a contract, Alfie. My son for one of your daughters, and you have two."

"It has been agreed that Louisa will be that girl," Alfie said.

"Louisa is fucking every single soldier you have guarding her," Daniel said. "It's pathetic, and I'm not taking a wife like that. You want to insult the Solano name, and insist I marry her, then we'll leave here with the start of a war, but it will be known that Valenti is the cause. Not us."

He was playing with fire. Before they even left the house, Alfie Valenti could kill them all, but again, he wouldn't live long to embrace the victory. There would be trouble no matter what, and vengeance would rain on the city. No, he'd be foolish to even think of trying something like that.

"Natalie is not part of this lifestyle."

"Her name is Valenti. She's your daughter, and she's who I want. Louisa is a slut. If you didn't want to parade your daughters in front of me, Valenti, you shouldn't have invited her for Thanksgiving."

He saw Natalie's brothers were shocked. Clearly, they hadn't anticipated Natalie capturing anyone's attention. They had underestimated her pull.

"Is this going to be a problem, Alfie?" Frank asked.

"No. You're going to have to give me time. Natalie and I have an agreement—"

"She's a woman. She'll learn to fall in line. I'm not leaving here without this agreement signed and sealed, and a date arranged," Frank said.

Alfie stared at both men. He looked a little pale, and Daniel saw his love for Natalie. "Go and get Natalie," he said, looking toward one of the soldiers at the door.

No one spoke as they all waited for Natalie to arrive.

"What the hell are you doing?" Vincent asked, leaning in close.

"What I want," Daniel said. They were used to their father telling them what to do, and how to live their lives. He was done playing that game. He was more than happy to marry. At thirty years old, he'd done all the playing around he needed to do, and now he wanted to move on. Starting a family didn't sound like a bad idea. When he imagined Natalie swollen with his child or running around the garden with a little boy or girl, it filled him with so much pride. No one had ever made him feel this way.

Natalie was special, and there was no way in hell that he was going to let her go.

The door opened, and he turned to see Natalie enter with a smile. She'd been chatting with the guard, completely unaware of what was about to happen.

The apron she wore was completely covered in flour, and there was some chocolate on her cheek, and her hair had other white powder in it. He didn't know what it was, but she looked utterly adorable.

When she saw all the men the smile on her face dropped. She wasn't an idiot, and he saw that.

"Hey, Dad," she said.

Her brothers were smirking, and Daniel wanted to protect her from their cruelty. This family, if it wasn't for the love he saw on Alfie's face, he'd happily start a war and slaughter them all in the name of Natalie.

As it was, Alfie looked ready to throw up, which was saying a lot.

After a few seconds, it fell away, and Alfie got his shit together, staring at his daughter. "You're to be married to Daniel," Alfie said.

"What?"

"You heard me."

"No, no, he's marrying Louisa. Would you like me to go and get her?"

"He doesn't want Louisa. It's you he wants."

Her gaze went to him, and he saw the fear there. She needed to be taught how to keep her emotions in check. People would walk all over her if she let them, and he had a feeling she did, often.

She shook her head. "No. You promised. We had an agreement, and you promised. I'm not a Valenti." Tears filled her eyes.

"This is the way it has to be. You and Daniel will be married. You will stop this ridiculousness, and you will become a Valenti bride." Alfie turned his attention to him. "Sign!"

Daniel stood, signing his name at the bottom of the contract.

Alfie turned to look at Natalie. "Sign it."

"No! You can't make me."

Alfie looked toward one of her brothers. They

suddenly left.

"Natalie, this is not a bad thing."

"We agreed," she said. "I asked you how I could get out of this, and since I was sixteen years old, I've been working for my living, and pulling away from the Valenti. I've done everything you've asked, and now you're taking it all away."

The tears stayed in her eyes, but he saw how hard it was for her. He felt so sorry for her, but Daniel knew he'd get her in the end. She'd be his wife, and he intended to treat her with love and respect, which was more than she'd get from a lot of men.

Her assumed name didn't matter. People would find out the truth, and then she'd end up dead.

The door to the office opened, and they pulled in Mary, the cook. The brother had a gun pointed at Mary's head, and Natalie gasped, going toward them.

"I will shoot her," her brother said. "Sign the damn paper."

"Mary?" Natalie asked. She shook her head. "I don't want to."

"It's okay, child."

Natalie's tears finally fell down, and she gasped on a sob. Pushing past everyone, she went to the desk and signed her name. "Let her go." She threw the pen down onto the desk.

The brother let Mary go, and Natalie rushed toward her friend.

She wouldn't look at any of them, and without a word, she left. She didn't even look toward her father.

Daniel didn't like the pain he saw on her face.

"Did you have to do that?" Daniel asked.

"Get over yourself," the brother said. "Natalie thinks she's too good for everyone. It's about time she was taught a lesson."

Daniel glared at him.

"This is done," Alfie said.

"Friday," Daniel said.

"What?"

"That's when I want all the arrangements made. This Friday, Natalie will be my wife, and we'll even have the wedding here. I don't think she's going to be so agreeable to a church wedding."

With that, he stood, leaving the room. Vincent and Ronnie flanked him.

"You took a risk in there," Ronnie said.

"Yeah, well, I've got what I want."

"You really want the girl or are you just fucking around?" Vincent asked.

"I want Natalie. She's going to be mine."

There's no way he could settle for second-best. He wanted Natalie, every single part of her from her sexy curves to her wonderful mind. He'd claim and take everything that she was. If she'd not turned up for Thanksgiving, this would have gone a lot differently.

****

Natalie couldn't remember crying so much in her life. No matter what Mary said to try to console her, the pain just kept coming back. She'd refused her father's invitation to not only join him for dinner but also to see him at all. She wanted nothing to do with him. He wasn't her family.

They'd had an agreement, and for business, he'd completely broken it.

Like her mother, who took a great deal of glee in what happened, said, she was just a woman, and in this world, she had no place. She was merely a pawn to be used, and that hurt more than anything else.

She was more than aware of what her family was capable of. Staring out of the window on the day of her wedding, she saw all the people getting ready. Her sister had already stopped by, smirking as she did, and said that if she tried to upset anyone, Mary would be dead. They were using Mary to make her conform.

Gripping the curtain, she wanted to scream, to curse, to do anything that would get her out of this.

Killing herself would get her out of what was about to happen, but she … couldn't do that.

She didn't want to die.

There was a soft knock on the door, and she didn't even bother to tell them to come in.

Glancing over her shoulder, she saw her father enter the room.

She couldn't look at him without feeling betrayed. No one else was in the room with her. She didn't have any bridesmaids, unless they counted her sister, who had appointed herself in that role. She didn't want anyone around her.

"Natalie…"

"You know, I could take the hatred from my brothers and Louisa. I could even handle Mom's utter contempt for me. I still don't know what I did wrong really. From what I can gather, she hated me before I even left the womb, so not a lot working there. Why?" she asked, looking toward him.

"It's business, Natalie."

She scoffed and gripped the curtain harder. "This is not business. I begged you not to bring me into this, and yet, here I am. On my wedding day with a man I don't know. I don't love him."

"Love is overrated."

"You never loved Mom?"

"Nope. I still don't. Haven't you ever wondered why your mother tried to kill you? She didn't want to be my wife, and I didn't want her. She planned to get rid of you, did you know that? I stopped her. Made sure that she couldn't take matters into her own hands. Forced her on bed rest, 'round the clock security, I even had to force feed her. There was no way I was going to let her kill something that belonged to me, and you're my daughter, Natalie. I should have known you were going to be different. You always have been. I had every intention of keeping our deal." He stepped up toward her. "Daniel is a good man. He will do everything to protect you."

"No, you see him as a good man because you can't stand the thought that you could be giving me to a monster. I don't need protecting from anything." She'd seen some of these "good men," and also the bruises that their wives tried to hide when there was a big party or something.

She placed a hand to her stomach.

Sickness kept sweeping through her, and it was scary.

It had been a long time since she was so scared.

"Honey, I would never give you to a man that is known to hurt women. Daniel isn't known for that. He's part of this life, I grant you, but he's not someone who hurts people for the fun of it. This is to stop a war."

"Marriage stops wars?"

"Yes. It keeps us all in line."

"Is that why you married Mom?" she asked.

"Yes."

There was no hesitation. "Did you ever love her?"

"No. I'm not like Daniel though, Natalie. He will learn to love you."

"I don't want to do this," she said. Tears built once again. She shook her head, refusing to let them fall. She wouldn't cry. Not now. Not ever.

Her father gripped her shoulders and pulled her against him. She went this time, not fighting him. What was the point? He'd win. The life she had planned, or at least hoped for, she realized was a dream. Her father would have never allowed it. He probably had something set up to keep her safe or some plan that kept her within the family. Her father always had a reason for doing everything.

"It's time for us to go down."

Even though she didn't want to go, and all she wanted to do was fight him, she didn't. She walked down to where her sister waited for her. The smug look on her face was almost too much.

Louisa had been basking in telling her exactly what she'd be involved with this evening. The lovemaking.

Natalie figured she'd let her sister have her fun, even though she knew every single word coming out of her mouth was a lie. Women didn't bleed profusely on the first time. There *was* a chance that Daniel would hold her down, and take what he wanted, but she didn't know.

Everything else, the searing pain that felt like fire, she knew was bullshit. Not only had she read up on it, but she had also checked some videos online. Yep, to help her this evening, she'd watched some porn, and while some stuff had been exceedingly disturbing, some hadn't.

Still, she didn't know what to expect from Daniel tonight.

She'd live through it.

She'd been able to live through her mother's attempts on her life, so she'd be able to live through pretty much everything else.

Louisa took the lead, heading toward the altar that had been set up.

She hadn't looked there yet, as she was too afraid. Biting her lip, she ran a hand down the front of her dress.

Her heart raced.

"I love you, Natalie. Please, never forget that," Alfie said.

Holding onto his hand, she finally lifted her head. Both of their families were there on either side of the aisle.

The wedding song came on, and slowly, too slowly, she was walked down the aisle. When she couldn't stand to look at the family and friends, she turned her attention to Daniel. He stood waiting for her.

His blue gaze captured hers, and for a few seconds, she felt completely lost. He seemed to ground her, and everything felt amazing. A rush ran through her, and as he smiled at her, she couldn't help smiling back.

This was utterly crazy, and yet, she didn't fight it. She went with it.

Her father placed her hand in Daniel's, and he led her toward the priest.

Staring down at their joined hands, she couldn't believe this was happening. Part of her wanted to run away, to scream for help.

No one would come, and so before their two families, she married Daniel. The next man in line to take over the Solano name.

When it came to the part of him kissing her, she had a little panic attack. Mary had trained her well, so instead of pulling away and screaming, she held herself still as he placed his lips against hers. His hand sank into her hair, and within seconds, she found herself responding to the pressure of his kiss.

It felt … good. So good.

He pulled away, and she heard clapping. People were happy to see them together. Daniel kept hold of her hand as they made their way toward the man with the camera. Of course, everything went off without a hitch.

They had pictures to be taken.

"You don't have to keep on holding me," she said.

"I'm going to keep on holding you for the rest of my life, baby," he said.

"Why?" she asked, looking up at him. No one was around, so they couldn't hear either of them talking. For a few blissful moments, they were alone.

"Why what?"

"Why me? Why didn't you pick Louisa? She's beautiful, and knew the score of what was expected of her."

He cupped her cheek, tilting her head back. His thumb lightly stroked, and she didn't like how easy it seemed to be distracting her.

"I didn't want her. I'm not here to have a woman who thinks of nothing but clothes and gossip. I like you, Natalie, and you may not think this, but I'm going to give you an amazing life."

She didn't say anything.

From the cameras, they were led toward the small feast. She couldn't believe how fast everything was set up. Selling off a daughter was clearly a regular feature in the mafia. She'd known it happened often, but still, she couldn't believe that *she* was the one that ended up sitting in this seat.

When the time came for them to have the first dance, she tried to pull away, but he wouldn't let her. Daniel was determined for her to keep doing every single step. By the end of the night, she'd learned they were no longer staying at her parents' house for their wedding night, which was news to her.

With his friends around them, he told her father that he was taking her home, to his home. She didn't want to leave, but holding her father a little too tightly, she knew there was nothing he could do.

This was over now, and she hugged Mary last, holding the woman tightly.

"You'll be fine, sweet child."

"I love you."

"I love you too."

She left her family behind and went with the family she'd been joined with. There was no happiness here, just a duty.

Chapter Four

Daniel said his goodbyes to his friends at the door. Vincent and Ronnie didn't have much to say back to him. They all knew that Natalie didn't want to be here. She'd not spoken a word to him in the car, or to anyone else. She had withdrawn into herself. He'd asked Mary about her often over the past week, finding the cook a valuable source of information when it came to his wife.

Natalie was hurting, and rather than explode she pulled her anger and fear inwards, not allowing it to show. He was upset that she didn't trust him with this.

Closing the door, he found her standing at the windows. The Solanos only dealt with luxury, so his apartment was the best that money could buy.

"This was a gift on my eighteenth birthday," he said, holding his key.

She didn't turn around to look at him. "Must have been nice."

"You didn't get a present on your eighteenth? I thought everyone did." He was trying to make light of everything.

"My dad came to my graduation and gave me a thousand dollars for my new life. I'd already been living by myself as part of our agreement. It felt like the best gift in the world because he accepted what I wanted." She finally turned to look at him, and he didn't like the pain in her eyes. "I should have known it wouldn't last. Women are disposable, right? You can get us anywhere."

"I don't think you're disposable."

"I never got that though. I mean, sure, men are strong, and normally assholes who think it's there right to rule the world, and women are just there to look pretty or to screw, when in fact, if women turned around and said screw it, the entire race would cease to exist."

"That would be cutting your nose off to spite your face."

"Women wouldn't do that though. You see, women know and understand that you need men and women. We're equal. It's just men that can't seem to want to share that kind of power." She shrugged. "Sorry."

"No, it's fine. You tell me everything you want to say."

"There's a lot I want to say that I'm not going to. I'm not good at this." She looked nervous, and he hated that.

Stepping up close to her, he took her hands and pulled her close. Their dance together had been so wrong, so there in his sitting room, he placed a hand on her back and took her other in his, resting it against his chest.

"What are you doing?"

"You need to relax. Nothing bad is going to happen."

She tensed again, and he cursed. No matter what he did, he couldn't win with this woman. It was starting to drive him insane, and they'd only been married a matter of hours.

He reminded himself that she didn't want this.

"I thought you looked incredibly beautiful today."

"Thank you."

Daniel liked her so damn much, and that thought alone scared him. He wasn't used to liking anyone, and yet, with her, he did. She was so beautiful, so tempting, and amazing. She didn't see her own charm.

He didn't like that she compared herself to Louisa a lot. From his talks with Mary, he discovered there was no love lost between the two. Natalie had tried to make friends with Louisa long ago, but it never happened. If anything, it made her life harder as Louisa would often mock her attempts.

"I want us to be friends, Natalie. To make a chance at this."

"Have you ever been friends with a woman?"

"Yes. Lots of times."

"That you've not had sex with?"

He sighed. "There's not a lot of chance to have something like that in the lifestyle we have."

"Nope, you're right."

"Are you a virgin?"

And like that, he ruined everything.

She tensed up and tried to pull away from him. "Let me go."

"I'm not going to hurt you."

"You just want to know if I'm a virgin. Yes, I am. I've not been with another man. Does that make you happy?"

Fear flashed within her gaze. He was much stronger than she was, so he pulled her against him, holding her close. "I'm not going to hurt you."

He cupped her face, tilting her head back, staring into her brown eyes. He'd never thought brown eyes were all that beautiful until that moment. When it came to Natalie, she really made him think and feel, and fuck! He didn't want to. His father had been pissed when he pulled that stunt in Alfie Valenti's office, but Daniel wouldn't budge. He didn't want to marry a woman he couldn't stand.

In their life, he'd seen it done so often. The women miserable as fuck, the men screwing around, taking whatever they could get from someone else, while hurting the woman that bore their name.

He wouldn't do that to Natalie. In the few hours he'd spent with her, he'd had more than an entire lifetime of fucking faceless women. For all of his thirty years, he'd followed instruction. He'd done everything that was demanded of him.

Only this once had he done what he wanted without looking back. Natalie was his reward as far as he was concerned. He'd never hurt her. He'd never take from her what wasn't freely offered. She didn't know him yet, and he hated that she was scared.

Tears glistened in her eyes, and she didn't believe him.

"Consummating the marriage?" she said. She spoke through gritted teeth, and he shook his head.

"They don't have to know. We're not going to do that tonight," he said.

She frowned.

"When we fuck, it's going to be because you want it, not me taking what's mine."

She looked so confused.

He was a monster in every single sense of the word, but tonight, he refused to be.

"Tonight, we're going to dance, and enjoy the fact we're married, and we're going to take our time getting to know one another." Anyone else could have thrown her to the bed and demanded their rights there and then. He wasn't like that. He didn't want to take from her. He wanted Natalie to give to him. She didn't relent at first, and he didn't mind. Holding her hand close to his heart, he closed his eyes and simply waited for her to finally melt against him.

It didn't take long before she did as he asked. The moment she did, it was a precious and beautiful thing, one he didn't want to let go of.

"You're a little strange. Anyone ever tell you that?" she asked.

He'd take whatever she wanted to talk about.

"I think being in this world, you've got to be a little strange. Especially this life. It's not for the fainthearted."

"No, I don't imagine it is."

"I don't always like it, if that's what you're asking."

She tilted her head back to look at him. "You don't get off on the power that you have within your grasp?"

He shook his head. "I don't get off on anything, baby. It's not who I am. Not now, not ever. I do what has to be done. It's what I was born to do."

"You guys have a lot more freedom than the women."

"I get that. We're allowed to have a time where we can play around, get everything out of our system to settle down."

"While the women can be passed around from the moment they're eighteen years old. A lot of girls are already sold in the name of peace and deals before they're even sixteen."

"Marriage never happens before they're eighteen though."

"Doesn't make it right. I wonder how the men would fare if the women went out, screwed around. Found random men to slake their thirst on. I doubt it would be all that much for all of you."

He smiled. "Louisa seemed to be doing a fine job of it. I saw the way that kid was looking at her."

"The soldier?"

"Yep. It wasn't hard to see. I'm surprised your father didn't."

"He has other things on his mind."

"Keeping a war from being unleashed is exhausting."

This time she giggled. "Louisa has always been a handful. I'm sure he's pissed that you didn't take her off his hands."

"Do you think he'd have given her the same consideration as you? Letting you go?" he asked, curious.

She shook her head. "Louisa wouldn't have been able to deal with the hard work. It's not inside her to break a nail over something as trivial as doing the dishes."

"You've not had a problem with it."

"I preferred to spend my time with Mary rather than my own mom, Daniel. She was a lot nicer to me, and she wanted me around. Also, the bonus, she didn't try to kill me."

He stroked the base of her back. "I don't want anyone to ever hurt you. I won't let them."

"I hate to be the party pooper here, Daniel, but if someone really wanted to, you couldn't really stop them."

****

Natalie didn't even know why she was talking about this. She had wanted to be the horrible woman, keeping Daniel at arm's length, making him wish he'd not picked her, but he was proving to be difficult to ignore. Not only did he make her feel safe and secure within his arms—and he did—but there was something … amazing about him.

He wasn't going to try to force her to sleep with him tonight, and she had been a little scared he'd do so.

The tales she'd heard were so damn scary.

Men raping their wives on the night or taking when they begged them not to.

Then of course all of Louisa's stories swirled around her head, and even though she knew they weren't true, once they were there, it was next to impossible to forget about them. It was driving her insane just thinking about it.

His thumb stroked her back, and she stared up at her.

"Haven't you realized anything yet, Natalie?" he asked.

"What is that?"

"That when I want something, I can be a very persuasive person."

"Agreed. You got my dad to back out of our agreement within a few minutes." She leaned back, smiling at him. She wasn't about to blame Daniel. He'd not wanted Louisa, and he'd done what he could to win her.

No, it was her father, refusing to step back and allow her to have her freedom that she blamed more than anything.

"Now that was the best victory of my life. I didn't think I'd be able to win that battle."

She chuckled. "You thought you had a battle on your hands?"

"Your father loved you. There wasn't a lot of love lost for Louisa. He wanted to protect you."

"The needs of the many far outweighed the needs of the few."

They both came to a stop when there was a knock on the door.

"Food?" he asked.

"We ate at the wedding."

"Nah, we didn't eat. We were both pushing food around our plates, and I'm not interested in all that fancy party stuff." He released her, and Natalie refused to think of how lonely she felt not having his arms wrapped around her. It didn't mean anything, not to her.

Still, she couldn't help but miss him. She hugged herself, watching as he opened the door.

Ronnie and Vincent stepped in, along with the sweet, amazing scent of Chinese food. Her stomach rumbled.

She'd relaxed enough to finally feel hungry.

"Still alive then," Vincent asked.

"Yep, I am, and hungry too."

"Good. We came with lots of offerings," Ronnie said.

They all sat down in the living room. Natalie took a seat on the floor, crossing her legs. The wedding dress spread out around her. Some of her hair was escaping the pins that had been keeping it in place.

Ignoring everything that was out of place, she grabbed a carton and a pair of chopsticks, and began to enjoy the delicious food. She loved Chinese food, but seeing as Mary cooked everything, she rarely got this treat anymore. It was an expense she couldn't afford.

"So, how is married life treating you?" Vincent asked.

She looked up, slurping some noodles. "Can't complain. We've only been together for a couple of hours."

Daniel had come to sit next to her, and every now and then, she chanced a glance at him. He surprised her all the time. The few times they'd been together prior to his wanting to marry her, she'd enjoyed his company.

Mary had even warned her not to get stars in her eyes, that he was destined for someone else. Only now, he was *her* husband.

"Ignore them, they're going to try and stir up shit."

She giggled. "So, you're all best friends?" She looked at each of them.

Vincent and Ronnie smirked.

"Actually, we're his dad's bastards," Ronnie said, being the first to speak up.

Her mouth fell open, she was sure of it. What then added to the certainty was the way Daniel reached over and closed it. She was thankful she didn't have any food in her mouth at the time.

"You're Frank's love children?" She looked among the three of them, seeing the similarities.

"My father is a real hero. We're all the same age."

"He knocked three women up at the same time?"

"Yep," Vincent said.

"My mom was the lucky one," Ronnie said. "She wasn't part of the life, so she didn't have to deal with his ass all that much."

"This is crazy. How are you guys like not angry about this? Daniel's the oldest, and that makes you guys the oldest."

"We share a birthday. We're all the same age, and Daniel is the son with the name. We don't hold the name," Vincent said. "No biggie. We're Daniel's protectors."

"They're my brothers and my best friends. I wouldn't let anything happen to them," Daniel said.

She saw the love among them, and she was a little jealous at how close they were. "I wish I had that. Louisa couldn't stand me. I don't make friends easily."

Her cheeks heating, she looked down at her food.

"As it happens we all make amazing friends. We'd gladly take you under our wing, show you the ropes of friendship."

She couldn't help but look toward Daniel.

He held his hands up. "I've not got a problem with this. When we're around the elders though, try to ignore them."

"Yes, it would seem elders don't like bastard children having a place," Ronnie said, winking at her.

"I'm so sorry," she said.

"You're really not a mafia brat, are you?" Vincent asked.

"I never really fit in. No, probably not. I guess having your mom trying to kill you on more than one occasion would do that to you."

She saw that she'd shocked them all.

"She tried to kill you?" Ronnie asked.

Nodding, she took a bite of her noodles. "A couple of times. I think it's why Dad was so nice to me. He didn't like that she tried to kill me." She shrugged.

They all finished their food, and she loved the time spent with them, but of course, it wasn't long before they had to leave, and the nerves kicked in.

She didn't know why she felt nervous.

Daniel had told her he wouldn't do anything with her unless she wanted it, and she didn't know if she wanted it or not.

Gathering up the empty cartons, she placed them in the trash and waited.

Sitting down on the stool, her hands linked together, she watched him come back.

"Do you want to see our bedroom?" he asked.

Locking her fingers together, she stood up and followed him. His hand rested at the base of her back, and even as her heart thumped, she tried to ignore it.

Entering the large bedroom, she saw the bed, which looked imposing and huge.

"Where will I be sleeping?"

"Here, with me." She made to protest, but he simply kissed her lips, silencing any further refusal. "Nothing is going to happen tonight. Trust my word on that, but we share a bed, that is the final word on it."

"You can't be swayed?"

"Not with this I can't."

"Okay." She stared at the bed a final time, seeing there was no point in arguing. "Would you undo the zipper of my dress?" She presented him with her back.

Her stomach clenched as his fingers grazed her side. She closed her eyes, thankful that he couldn't see her.

"I know you're affected by me," he said, lips brushing her neck.

Opening her eyes, she stared at him. She'd been so drawn to the bed she'd not noticed all the mirrors.

"You like to watch something?" she asked, feeling her skin heat up.

"I like to do a lot of things, Natalie." The zipper slid down her back, easing open with each second.

His touch was light, and yet it set a fire within her.

He didn't let her go right away, drawing her back against him.

Staring at their reflections, he placed his hand over her stomach, the other taking hold of one of hers. "You're beautiful."

"Thank you."

"I'll never do anything to you that will scare you, okay."

"I believe you."

"I want this to work. I know you probably hate me for taking you away from a life you wanted, but I will make sure you don't regret it."

He kissed her neck and let her go.

She stepped into the bathroom. Staring at her reflection, she looked … a mess. Her hair was all over the place. Her wedding dress was falling down, but obviously, that was because he'd opened it.

"You can do this, Natalie. It's fine."

Taking a shower, she freshened up, taking care of her teeth afterward.

Wrapping a robe around her, she entered the bedroom and found a negligee waiting for her on the bed. With no sign of Daniel there, she quickly pulled it on and released the robe. Putting everything in the laundry basket, she returned to the bedroom and began to brush her hair, sitting at the vanity table.

Seconds later, Daniel entered. He wore a pair of pajama bottoms and nothing else. In the low lighting, everything seemed to stand out on his body, and it made her ache to see more.

He stepped up behind her, taking the brush from her. "May I?"

"Sure." He had the brush anyway.

Staying perfectly still, she watched as he brushed her hair. The locks were a little damp, and he was so gentle. It didn't take long for her to close her eyes and enjoy the way he brushed her hair.

You're totally losing it on this guy.

He didn't linger, and once her hair was brushed, he dropped a kiss to her shoulder.

There was no need to avoid it. She made her way toward the bed, being sure not to make eye contact with him. Climbing in, she snuggled into the comfortable bed, aware of how nice it felt.

Daniel slid in behind her, wrapping his arm around her waist and pulling her close. She didn't fight him.

At first, she was a little afraid. She wasn't used to sharing a bed with anyone. Slowly, she relaxed against him, enjoying the feel of his body against hers.

Closing her eyes, she found sleep.

Chapter Five

The following day, Daniel woke up and watched Natalie sleep. She was pressed up against him. Her hand was around his waist, her head against his chest. He didn't want to leave the bed, but his cell phone was ringing.

Slowly, he slid out from beneath her, wanting to kill whoever was calling him. This was his fucking honeymoon, period. He didn't even go away for a couple of weeks. Staring down at Natalie, he wished he'd fought a bit harder.

Gritting his teeth, he left the bed, padding across the room to take out his cell phone. He didn't linger in his bedroom and took the call.

It was his father.

"Hello," he said.

"We need you today," Frank Solano said.

"Seriously?"

"You can do what you need to do later. I need you in. Don't disappoint me."

The call ended, and he gritted his teeth. He was so fucking angry.

"Bad call?" Natalie asked.

He turned to find her leaning against the doorframe.

The negligee he'd picked out for her made him aware that he had a dick, and as he stared at her, it was getting a whole lot harder.

"Business."

"They want you to go in?"

"Yes."

She nodded and stepped away. "That's okay."

He moved back into the bedroom and found her making the bed. "I have a cleaner who does that."

She stood up and glanced over at him. "I'm not going to be able to handle some stranger making my bed."

"You make beds now?"

"I also clean and cook. I guess you could consider me your new cleaner."

When she bent over the bed to fix a crease, he could only stand and admire. He thought about her in a maid's costume, showing off a fine curve of ass, and his cock was all ready to play this morning.

She stood up, and she turned toward him.

He'd not moved.

Her gaze moved down his body, and he knew his pants were tented because of his dick, but he didn't care.

She didn't say anything, just looking from his dick to his eyes.

Neither of them spoke or moved.

"You do breakfast?" he asked. He was going to prove to her that it didn't matter how aroused he was, he could control himself.

She nodded, running fingers through her hair.

"I'm using the bathroom," he said.

"O-okay."

He smirked at her and left the door partially open. Stepping into the shower, he put the water on, relishing the icy blast as it rained down on him.

The cold water did nothing for his erect cock, which pissed him off.

Wrapping his fingers around the length, he began to work his dick, up and down, going from the root up to the tip and back again. Placing another hand on the wall, he thought about Natalie, bent over the bed, her ass in the air, looking so inviting, and yet not even asking for attention.

Her subtle sexuality was like a drug to him. He

wanted more, and yet couldn't get any more. He always had to wait, to be patient.

He thought about her turning to face him, and instead of looking a little embarrassed at seeing his aroused state, she would remove her clothing, giving him the show of her nice big tits. The negligee would fall to the floor, and she'd step out of it.

She wouldn't try to hide.

No, she'd kneel before him, taking his pants down and wrapping her fingers around his length. The moment her hot mouth sucked on the tip, he'd be a goner, but he wouldn't let her off that easily. No, he'd take his sweet time, counting sheep if he had to in order to gain control.

Holding onto her hair, he'd guide his dick into her mouth, and she'd swallow him down, moaning as he did, going to the back of her throat.

Before he could finish, the first waves of his arousal crashed through him. The white streams of his cum spilled out, hitting the floor of the shower and washing down the drain. Even his own fantasies were against him, not allowing him to get to the end and to experience that sweet bliss, and it would definitely be bliss.

Resting his head against his hand, he watched the water run down the drain, giving himself a few seconds to gain control. Running a hand down his face to clear the last of the arousal, he turned off the shower and stepped out. Wrapping a towel around his waist, he entered the room.

Before he did, he frowned and took a step back into the shower. There in the basket was the negligee. At some point during pleasuring himself, Natalie had entered.

He wondered if she'd stayed.

Then his curiosity got the better of him, and he wondered how much she knew about sex. She'd tried to escape the life, but that didn't for a second mean she was a naive woman. A virgin, yes, but that didn't mean she was unaware of sex, fucking, the works.

He changed quickly and found Natalie in the kitchen. Ingredients were on the counter, and when she looked at him, she smiled, but he saw the hint of red in her cheeks.

"Morning," he said.

"Morning. Nice shower?" She shook her head. "Sorry. I … I was…"

"You saw me with my cock in my hand."

"You were … very vocal. I'm sorry. I tried not to look, and I don't usually stare."

"Did you enjoy what you saw?"

She bit her lip, and he wanted to kiss those lips. He didn't.

"Yes, I did," she said. "Does that surprise you?"

"It does, and I like it."

She placed a coffee in front of him. "Should we talk about this?"

When she made to pull away, he captured her hand, and pressed a kiss to her wedding ring. "We're husband and wife. I don't expect you to talk with anyone else but me."

"You've got no chance of me ever talking about this with anyone."

"Do you know what happens…." Now *he* couldn't finish.

"Yes, of course. I'm a virgin, Daniel. It doesn't mean I don't understand what sex is or what you have to do." She squeezed his hand and pulled away. "Won't your dad be angry with you for being late?"

"It's the day after my wedding. Most people get a

few days off. I'm sure spending the morning with my wife is fine." He winked at her.

If his father was pissed, he wouldn't let her know.

The doorbell rang, and he let Natalie keep on cooking breakfast while he went to answer it. Ronnie and Vincent were there, and they looked pissed. "We figured today was a day off," Vincent said, speaking up first.

"It was. It was supposed to be. I guess things are different for us." He shrugged and stepped back to let them in.

"What's that smell?" Ronnie asked.

"My wife is cooking. It smells good."

"She cooks?" This from Vincent.

"Cleans too. She doesn't want a stranger in her home cleaning her bed."

"She's a keeper," Ronnie said.

They headed back to the kitchen. There Natalie stood at the stove, flipping bacon on the pan. She wore an apron this time, which was a good thing as some of the bacon fat splattered on the front.

"I never thought I'd see a Valenti in the kitchen," Vincent said.

She turned toward them, a huge smile on her face, which twisted his heart. "I spent most of my years in the kitchen. Mary taught me a thing or two. She probably shouldn't have, but I happen to like being there. Take a seat. There's plenty for everyone."

"Of course there is," Daniel said.

"You've got enough food in here to feed an army. I hate to think of this going to waste if you don't eat it, and they look hungry."

Vincent and Ronnie stood together, touching their stomachs.

Daniel burst out laughing and rolled his eyes. "I didn't say you couldn't feed them. Be careful, or they'll be here all the time."

Taking his coffee, he looked at her a final time, wishing he could stay with her, but took it to the table where they had some privacy.

"I want one of you to stay here, to keep her company," Daniel said, taking a seat.

Neither of them spoke as Natalie rushed inside, putting a coffee in front of each of them.

"I'll be back soon," she said.

He watched her go and wished he didn't have to leave her today. Something was happening between them, and he didn't want to leave her while he could help those feelings develop.

Ronnie and Vincent glanced at each other.

"I don't care who stays or who goes."

"Either way, one of you will be with her at all times. You can swap and change it if you'd like."

"I'll take first babysitting duty," Vincent said. "You want to split it by days or weeks?"

"Days. One day you're with her, next day I am." Ronnie turned to look at him.

"I want a full report though of everything that's going down. I won't be kept in the dark."

"Don't worry, we'll do that."

They all stopped talking as Natalie joined them. She placed their three meals in front of them.

Bacon, eggs, hash browns, and some tomatoes. It all looked so good.

She came back with her own breakfast and buttered bread.

Taking a slice of bread, she sat next to Ronnie, who immediately stood up. "You've got to sit next to the boss man. I insist."

She glanced at him, and he liked that she checked if it was okay with him.

"Yes, I want you to sit here."

Natalie took her place at his side. Vincent and Ronnie were giving him sly looks, but he didn't give a fuck. He couldn't spend the entire day with his woman, so he was going to take every opportunity he had to get close to her.

****

"So I'm not allowed to work anymore?" Natalie asked, staring at Vincent.

"That's right."

"You know, you get to work. I think this is a little unfair, and totally sexist."

Vincent was sitting at in the living room, reading a cooking magazine. "Be that as it may, what you do reflects on your husband. Working for your keep is not exactly going to go down well."

She rolled her eyes. "I like to work!" She flopped down on the sofa.

"Shopping is work?"

"I don't shop."

"Maybe we should try it?" he asked, looking at her. "Have you ever tried to shop?"

"Nope. I tend to avoid activities with people who hate me."

"I'm sorry about your mom trying to kill you."

"I got over it." She couldn't just sit down, so she stood and began to pace the living room. Everything sparkled so she couldn't even clean anything. She'd cleaned the kitchen twice already and reorganized the shelves.

She didn't like that another woman had an order inside her home.

The last thing she'd ever wanted was to get married to someone within the mafia, but now that she was, she wanted this to remain her home, and because of that, it meant she was going to have things the way she liked it.

Her apartment wasn't large. It was a modest one-bedroom, and she loved it.

Of course, since her impending wedding, she'd not been back there. Her father had demanded she stay at home until the wedding. The apartment had been cleared out and was probably leased out to someone else.

"Fine, let's go shopping. Let's go and do something, rather than be cooped up in this place."

She was used to doing everything and nothing. Sitting around all day waiting for Daniel to come home was not how she wanted to spend her days.

Humming to herself, she grabbed a jacket and her bag.

Vincent was already at the door, waiting for her.

"Whatever the lady wants," he said with a wink.

They walked toward the elevator and she sighed, leaning against the wall, waiting for it to move.

"I'm not good at this," she said.

"Being the lady of leisure?"

"Yes. I couldn't stand sitting in the kitchen and doing nothing. I just … I can't do it."

"It's fine. We'll see how shopping is for you."

The elevator opened to the underground parking lot. When Vincent went to open the door to the back passenger seat, she shook her head. "Not a chance."

"You're going to be a modern mafia lady, huh?"

"Nope. I'm going to be myself."

Climbing into the front seat, she buckled in, and waited as Vincent did the same, only he turned over the ignition.

"Let's get this show on the road."

He pulled out of the underground parking lot, and the moment she was away from the apartment, she felt a million times better.

"I'm so pleased right now," she said. "Will you be the one taking care of me?"

"Not all the time. Between Ronnie and myself, we'll keep you safe."

"I don't get a soldier?"

"Daniel would only trust your safety with one of us."

"Do you wish you weren't his brother?" she asked, turning to look at him.

Vincent shook his head. "There's nothing about Daniel's life I crave. At least being the bastard, I don't have to be ordered around. For the most part, Frank wants nothing to do with me. My mom wants nothing to do with my dad. It works."

"It must have been … hard."

"Not really. Daniel's not an asshole, and being friends with him, it's not hard either. We all want the same thing. I'd die for that little shit," he said with a smile. "I know he'd die for me. That in itself is the problem."

"How is it?"

"We're just the bastards while he's the king."

She swallowed the lump in her throat. "This world is cruel."

"I can't deny that. It's not the easiest world to live in, but it's our world."

Natalie stared out at the street, watching ordinary people pass through their lives, looking so normal.

"I always wished I was one of them," she said, pointing out at the street. "Completely oblivious to the world around them."

"They have it easy to a point, Natalie. They've all got problems though. Being in the mafia doesn't exactly mean your life is over." He pointed at people. "Her father could have abused her. His mother could have beaten him as a child. Someone on these streets could have been a loser, and be wanting to stalk a woman to kill her? They're not free. Does it make their vices worse because they are civilians?"

She shrugged. "I don't know. I didn't think of it like that."

"Can I ask you a question?"

"Sure."

"Do you like Daniel?"

This made her pause, and she looked at Vince. They had stopped at a traffic light. "I don't really know him."

"But you like him?"

"I … this is hard. He seems nice … and he's been very accommodating." She felt like a bitch. "Yes, I like him. I didn't want to, and for the past week, I did kind of hate him."

He chuckled. "None of us expected him to demand you. That was news to us."

"I don't even know what I did to gain his attention, you know? I'm just me, and we just talked. Nothing actually happened."

"From what I know, you talked to him, and you spoke about things that were more than fashion and gossip. You didn't care about who was screwing who, or what that meant for you. You didn't talk about purses or jewelry."

She talked about everything else.

"You didn't look scared of him either, or see him as an easy target. You treated him like an ordinary guy."

"Because I'm an ordinary girl."

"Regardless of what you were trying to achieve, Natalie, you are and will always be a Valenti. That in itself means you were no ordinary girl. Say he hadn't taken your hand in marriage, and you married someone who wasn't aware of this life. You could have gotten him killed. If someone wanted to make a statement, a guard close by wouldn't stop it. What would you have done then? Not only would you be dead, but so would someone else. Daniel does what he has to. You've picked a damn good guy, and you should be proud. He'd never hurt you, or allow anything to happen to you."

Chapter Six

"How are things going with the girl?" Frank asked.

"It's been one day. Things are going good." Daniel watched as his father leaned back. He'd just watched as Frank tortured a rat, trying to find out where the leak of information was coming from, and they thought they'd finally found it.

Even with his shirt covered in blood, Frank was happy. No one commented, not one maid, as they flitted around the room, cleaning up after him. This was the Solano way. Everyone expected Frank to come home looking a mess, and no one ever commented.

"I want her pregnant as soon as possible."

Daniel stared at his father.

"What?"

"You heard me. I don't want to wait or give the Valentis a reason to think they can pull out of our alliance. I want her knocked up immediately. I'm giving you the next month off. Do what needs to be done. Remember what I've taught you, and I don't want you to disappoint me, Daniel. I mean that."

With a wave of his hand, Frank dismissed him.

Getting to his feet, Ronnie followed him out of the room. Neither of them spoke, waiting until they got in the car to finally say something.

Climbing behind the wheel, Ronnie started the car up, and they left his father's estate before even speaking a word.

"What are you going to do?" Ronnie asked.

He'd confided in his friends that he'd not taken Natalie, letting them know that he wanted her to fall in love with him before anything took place.

Sitting back, he rubbed his eyes.

"Do you think he's got cameras in my home?" Daniel asked.

"I'm starting to think he might have because there's no way in hell that he can expect you to do just as he says."

"He's the boss, of course he can."

"If you hurt Natalie, force yourself on her, she'll never forgive you."

"I don't do rape, Ronnie. That will never change." He ran a hand down his face. This was not what he wanted to deal with right now.

They didn't make a single stop and arrived at his penthouse suite quickly. He noticed Vincent's car was missing, and he pulled out his cell phone.

Daniel: **Where r u?**

Vincent: **shopping, or at least trying to. Your wife is weird.**

Daniel smiled, thinking about his wife. She wasn't the kind that would love to spend the entire day shopping, not at all.

"Come on, we've got some time to check my place."

Ronnie went to the trunk of his car, where he found the piece of equipment that would say if there was a bug in his home.

He hoped to God there wasn't. Right now, he didn't want to have to deal with the thought of his father listening in on his conversations. That would piss him the fuck off.

Once again, neither of them spoke, entering his apartment, and the moment they did, they began to search.

Within the space of twenty minutes all of the bugs were found and he placed them on the counter, pissed off.

They were still live, and right now he didn't know what to do with them.

Grabbing Ronnie's arm, he pulled him toward the bedroom, the only place they hadn't found one.

"He knew," Ronnie said.

"There's no other word for it. He knew what you said, and this is some kind of test."

Daniel ran fingers through his hair.

He'd known his father liked to randomly do surveillance, but this was just fucking out of line.

"Why do you think he's doing this?" Ronnie asked.

"I don't know. Knowing him, it's one of his power trips, where he likes to completely control fucking everything!" He wouldn't do it. No matter what his father wanted, he wouldn't rape Natalie.

This wasn't the reason he picked her in place of Louisa. He liked Natalie. He didn't think he'd have to convince Louisa to get into his bed, but still, he couldn't bring himself to stick his dick inside her.

"Honey, we're home," Vincent said, calling out to them.

Daniel gritted his teeth.

Entering the main room, he smiled at Vincent, and raised a brow when he caught sight of his very sexy, beautiful wife, in a pair of jeans and a shirt, bending over and plugging in a lamp.

There were a couple of large bags, and Vincent looked mildly amused.

"So your lady wouldn't go with the clothes shopping, and she wanted to put her touch on the apartment. Decided that this is her place, and it will be like it."

"Speaking of it being part of my place," Natalie said, coming toward him. She pushed some hair off her face. "How good are you at fixing things?"

"What kind of things?"

"You know, assembling a bookcase."

Before he could say anything, two delivery men entered the apartment, and Natalie gave a squeal of excitement.

"Yay!"

He watched as a large box was placed on the floor.

"I've never done one before, and I was hoping you strong men could get it done for me while I fix some dinner." She tilted her head to the side, looking all coy and adorable, and fuck, he adored her.

She inspired feelings inside him that no other woman had.

"We'll get it fixed."

Ronnie cleared his throat and did some weird eye movement. For a few seconds, he'd forgotten the pressing problem.

Daniel crooked his finger to Natalie, and she stepped toward him. He pointed a finger to his lips, letting her know to be quiet.

With that, he led her toward the equipment, and he saw she knew what it was.

Pointing toward the bedroom, Vincent and Ronnie followed.

"That's not gross at all. Who put listening devices in your apartment?" Natalie asked.

"First, how do you know what they are?"

"I've seen something similar from my dad. He told me how they work, even let me listen in once. Big mistake. Whoever he was listening to was having sex. Believe me, a ten-year-old doesn't need to hear that. Or 'hit me again, baby, make it hurt.'"

Ronnie and Vincent were trying to contain their

laughter, and he wasn't having much good at it either.

"My dad," he said.

He nodded at Ronnie and Vincent, and they left the room. Seconds later he heard the door close, and figured Ronnie was giving Vincent the update.

Daniel sat on the end of the bed and sighed.

"Your father is listening in on you. Doesn't he trust you?"

"I don't know. It's my dad, and it's his way of keeping control of everything."

She took a seat beside him. "It didn't go well? This meeting with him? Your business."

"I'm going to be completely honest with you, because I don't want any secrets between us."

"Okay."

"My dad wants me to get you pregnant as soon as possible."

"ASAP?"

"Yes."

"Oh."

He took hold of her hand, locking their fingers together. "He must have heard what I said to you."

"Yeah, because that's not creepy at all."

"I never claimed to have a perfect family."

"Neither have I." She squeezed his hand and offered him a smile. "You don't have to look terrified." She chuckled and winked at him.

"He's given me a month to do it."

"Oh, wow, he doesn't want you wasting any time."

"I think it's some kind of test."

She didn't look shocked by that. "Our fathers and all these tests. It's probably to help cement the Solano-Valenti deal or whatever you guys got out of this marriage. I don't really know."

"I only wanted you, Natalie."

She smiled and took her hand back. He watched as she ran her hands down her thighs. "There's not a lot we can do then, right? You're being honest with me, and let's face it, you can't exactly get rid of those devices. This room is clear?"

"Yes."

She nodded. "Then we're going to have to ... you know ... have sex."

"Are you even ready for a baby?"

She shook her head. "I'm not, but I also know how these things go, and believe me, they never end well for people who completely disregard an order." She stood up. "I'm going to fix some dinner for us all. I suggest you get Vincent and Ronnie and put them back. We'll know where they are. We know where our privacy is, and we'll just have to deal with it."

"I'm a full-grown man."

"I know." She reached out, touching his cheek. "I never said it makes it right. Families always do crazy things."

He watched her walk away.

He was pissed off that his father would do this. What Daniel wanted to know was why?

****

Flossing her teeth had never seemed like such an important thing to do, and yet here she was, standing at the bathroom sink, running white cotton things through her teeth. Natalie had already showered and brushed her teeth twice. Now she decided she needed to floss. She wore a negligee, one that Daniel had purchased for her.

Tonight she was going to lose her virginity, and she didn't know how she felt about that.

Sex was something she'd wanted but hadn't craved it.

Why crave something she hadn't really been *that* interested in?

With her teeth flossed and her hair brushed with about two hundred strokes, she couldn't think of any other reason to remain in the bathroom.

Grabbing a cloth, she wiped down the bathroom sink, even though it was spotless. She made a note to ask Daniel if he'd canceled the woman he normally had for cleaning.

"Everything is fine." She stared at her reflection, hating the fear staring back at her.

Her father had once said if someone was listening in, it didn't mean good things for the future.

Were both of their fathers listening in?

She didn't know, and she didn't want to know.

The thought of her father invading her privacy like that was just too much for her to handle. She refused to think like that, and she stepped away from the sink. There was no point in putting this off any longer.

Staring down at her wedding band, she couldn't believe that she'd been married a whole day. That was all it was, and yet when she was around Daniel, it felt like much longer. Not because he was a pain in the ass or anything, just the way they were together.

Entering the bedroom, she saw Daniel wore a black robe, and he was sitting on the edge of the bed.

She smiled at him. He looked troubled.

"You were in there a long time," he said.

"I was … trying to distract myself. It's not every day that a woman loses her virginity or anything. Or finds out that her father-in-law likes to keep track of her conversations."

She tried to make light.

Daniel sighed. "I'm a thirty-year-old man, and I've been ordered to fuck my wife and knock her up."

She winced. "Have you been a good boy?"

They both laughed.

"I'm sorry. I didn't know of a good way to phrase it, and words are not always my strong suit."

She stepped up to where he sat. She held out her hands, and he took them, and she stared at where they were joined once again.

"I won't ever hurt you, regardless of what anyone wants from me. You wanted out of this life, and I brought you back in. For that, I am truly sorry."

"There wasn't a lot you could have done." She paused. "You could have fallen for Louisa, and that would have been … easier. Oh, well, life is never easy, is it? Not really."

He stood up, and she held in her gasp.

He was so much taller than she was, bigger, and when he moved closer to her, she couldn't think, not for a second. His touch grazed up her hands, and she closed her eyes, feeling every little aftershock from his touch alone.

"I will only ever do what you want me to, Natalie."

She knew if she asked him to stop, he would. He wasn't a monster.

Daniel was a good man who did bad things because he had no choice.

The life he was born to decreed that.

When he cupped her face and tilted her head back, she didn't fight him. Her stomach tightened, and a flood of warmth filled her pussy. Her nipples tightened too, and when his lips finally touched hers, she couldn't resist the moan that escaped.

Daniel swallowed down her moan, holding her tightly as he explored her mouth. She closed her eyes, desperate for more, to feel him surround her. She didn't want him to stop.

Grabbing the belt of his robe, she tugged it open. Her hands met naked chest, and she ran them up, moving toward the arms of the robe, and sliding it off his shoulders.

The robe landed on the floor with a thud.

Breaking from the kiss, she saw that he hadn't worn any clothing, and he stood before her naked.

He was all hard muscle, covered in ink, and totally sexy as she stared at him. She couldn't believe for a second that this man belonged to her.

Biting her lip, she met his gaze.

"I figured undressing would make you more nervous."

She chuckled. Placing her fingers on the straps of her negligee, she didn't give herself a second to doubt her moves. When she slid the straps down her arms, the negligee fell down, landing at her hips. She gave a little wiggle, and the negligee fell to the floor.

Just as he stood naked before her, she stood before him, completely nude.

She couldn't help covering her breasts, crossing her arms together, hiding a little part of herself.

Daniel stepped forward, taking her hands, and pulling her close. As he eased her arms down, their chests collided, and she closed her eyes, wrapping her arms around his back as his hands touched hers.

Opening her eyes, she found their reflections in one of the many kinky mirrors that he had.

His hands caressed up and down her back, and she eased her head away to look at him.

"I trust you, Daniel."

He gripped her ass, and she felt the hard ridge of his cock poking against her stomach. She didn't fight him as he spun her around and moved her back to the bed.

When the backs of her legs hit the bed, and she dropped with a thud, she let out a little giggle.

As she lay back on the bed, all laughter ceased when he spread her legs open. The instant his hand touched her pussy, she gasped. Fire and pleasure danced together. Moving to her elbows, she glanced down between her thighs and watched as he teased through her slit, spreading the lips of her pussy and touching her clit. She gasped as he slid his fingers back and forth over her clit.

She arched up, needing more.

Daniel placed a hand on her stomach and pressed her down to the bed.

When his lips replaced her fingers, she didn't think for a second anything else could have felt so damn good.

His tongue, though, the way it danced and licked across her clit, she went to heaven.

Pleasure unlike anything she'd ever felt before began to build inside her, and she felt that point that she'd read about in so many books. She felt the precipice that he kept her at but wouldn't allow her to fall over.

She gritted her teeth, begging him to let her fall over the edge. Daniel was the one in control though, and only when he was ready for her to fall did he send her over, spiraling the pleasure, shocking her with the level of her climax.

Natalie didn't think it was possible to ever experience that kind of rapture, but she did at the ministrations of his tongue and hands.

She didn't want it to end.

The fire he ignited within her was like an inferno.

The moment he flicked the switch, she didn't want to turn back.

He eased off her pussy and moved over her.

Going on instinct alone, she cupped his face, kissing him. She didn't care about the taste of her pussy. All that she cared about was the feel of him around her. His hands moved up and down her sides, stroking her, showing her in more ways than one how good having him could be.

"Are you ready?" he asked, sliding between her thighs.

They'd moved up the bed, and he rested between her thighs, his cock against her pussy.

She licked her lips and nodded. "Yes, I'm ready."

His hand moved between them, his cock sliding down her slit to her entrance. She couldn't help but tense. In all the books she'd read it was such a cliché, and yet here she was, in the same predicament, and acting exactly the same way. She was twenty years old, and shouldn't be nervous.

Daniel slammed to the hilt inside her, and she cried out as the searing pain shook her to her core. She gripped his shoulders, shocked by the sudden invasion.

He wrapped his arms around her, staying still, and she couldn't believe that tears leaked out of her eyes.

This was not how she imagined her first time. She'd figured the pain was a lie, something to keep women in line. They weren't lying.

She held onto him, hoping his strength gave her strength.

"I'm sorry, baby," he said, kissing her shoulder.

His tenderness melted the last of the ice around her heart.

Chapter Seven

A couple of hours later, Daniel ran the sponge over her body. Natalie rested against him, and he smiled.

"I feel … weird," she said.

"Good weird, or bad weird?"

"I don't know. I mean, I thought about what it would all mean to lose my virginity. It's what a lot of people do."

"Nah, not for men. Unless of course they've not gotten rid of it by their late teens, and then it's an obsession."

She chuckled.

"How did you think it was going to go?" he asked, curious.

"I don't know. I didn't think there'd be as much pain as there was."

Daniel held her just a little tighter. When he closed his eyes, he saw and heard that little scream and the shock that entered her eyes as he'd slammed inside her. He'd felt her virginity break, tearing open as he claimed her for his own.

He liked that no other man had ever gotten to taste her, or to know how her pussy clenched around his cock. Every new sensation she had was all for him.

"I'm so sorry," he said.

The last thing he ever wanted to do was cause her pain, and yet he had.

She held onto his arm and smiled up at him. "I believe every woman has to go through that. You don't have to keep blaming yourself." She spun around and moved so that she straddled his waist. The bathtub was huge, so there was plenty of room for the both of them.

Resting his hands on her hips, he stared down at her body. He loved her curves, fucking relished them.

They tempted him in every single way, and he couldn't get enough of her.

He'd been more than prepared to wait. Even though his father had given him an instruction, he'd have waited.

Natalie meant more to him than getting the deed done.

"Just because there's supposed to be pain doesn't mean I love to give it."

"You're not a Dom then?"

"A Dom?"

"You know? The whole big thing of the moment with whips, chains, safewords."

He laughed. "No, and I'm surprised you know that stuff."

"I have a very wide collection of amazing books."

Daniel squeezed her ass. "Well, whatever the lady wants, I will be sure to make all of your dreams come true."

She moaned, and that amazing sound went straight to his cock.

Natalie nibbled her lip, and the teasing smile that she gave him made him think of all the things he wanted to do to her.

"You mean that?" she asked.

"Yes, I mean that. I want to give you everything your heart desires."

"And I want to do the same for you. Everything." The smile fell from her lips, and he didn't like that.

"Talk to me," he said. "This is not supposed to be a sad moment, but a happy one."

"We're married now, and even though I didn't originally want to, we're together."

"Yes, we are," he said in agreement.

"Well … forget it. I'm being stupid."

"You're not being stupid, and I may not be a Dom, but I am more than willing to spank this ass if you need it."

She chuckled. "Okay, fine, I don't want us to have a marriage like our parents did. I never wanted to be in a relationship where I was wondering if he was cheating or if he was happy. If he was thinking about another woman." She teased the hair at the back of his neck. "I don't want you to get a mistress or to cheat, or anything like that. I …when you want something like that, I want you to come to me, no matter what the time is, or the day, or whatnot. I want to be the woman that satisfies all of your needs. Every last one of them."

Her cheeks had gone a delightful pink.

"Do you want to be my living sex toy?" he asked.

He had no intention of being with anyone else, of going to another woman. That was not what he wanted.

Natalie was his, and he'd wait for however long she wanted him to get her.

Pushing some of her hair off her shoulder, he smiled. "If you're my sex toy, then I want to be yours."

"You want to be my dildo?" she asked.

"Yes. Every little desire, secret fantasy, let me know, and I will give it to you. We're here because of my father, but I picked you. There won't be another woman for me, Natalie. I don't want to be in a loveless marriage, or having to screw a wife out of necessity. I want everything, and I'm a greedy bastard."

"I don't mind you being greedy." She cupped his face. "I'm going to kiss you now."

"Then kiss me."

Her lips slammed down on his. At first her touch was a little unsure, but he didn't let her go. The kiss deepened, and he couldn't help closing his eyes, basking in her touch. She was like fire in his arms, and he never wanted to let her go.

Running his hands up her back, he deepened the kiss. Plunging his tongue into her mouth and hearing her moan had his dick pulsing in a fresh wave of arousal.

Her hand dropped from his face and moved between them, sliding around his cock.

He growled but didn't break the kiss. He didn't want to.

She ran her hand up and down the length, teasing him.

The water around them was going cold, but her touch was firing his blood.

"I want you," she said, breaking the kiss.

"Are you sore?"

"I don't care. I need you, Daniel."

He didn't have the patience to make it to the bed, and so lifting her up, he slowly eased her down onto his cock. Natalie guided the tip to her entrance, and once he was a few inches inside, she slammed down on his cock, shocking him.

She wrapped her arms around him as well as her legs, holding him tightly.

Gripping her hips, he began to rock inside her, guiding her, feeling her pelvis rub against him.

The pleasure was instant, and he fucking loved it. The only thing that would make this even better was if he had some mirrors to watch everything.

Reaching between them, he found her clit, and he refused to find his own release until she'd at least found hers.

Stroking her clit, he broke the kiss, watching her gasp. Her eyes dilated, and she fucked his cock as he kept up with his stroking.

Her tits bounced, and he was in heaven.

Her body was a fucking dream to him. He

couldn't get his fill of her, and she only served to arouse him more.

"I love fucking you, Natalie. You better get used to feeling my dick inside you, because that's all I'm going to want to do. Fuck you, take you, make you mine." He didn't want her to move without being reminded of him inside her.

She nodded. "Yes, please, Daniel."

"You want to come?"

"Yes."

"I want to hear you scream my name, and come all over my dick. I want you to make it wet, so fucking wet."

He stroked her clit, and she came.

Her cunt tightened around him, drawing his own release from him. She yelled his name, and he cried out hers as he kept on stroking her even though his release spilled from him, filling her cunt.

One day soon he was going to fill her, and it was going to stick. She was going to be full and swollen with his kid.

He loved the thought of that, and as they both came down from their peak he placed a hand across her stomach.

Her hand covered his. "Whatever happens, Daniel, our child will be *ours*, and you cannot let either of our fathers get to him or her. Are you wanting a son?"

"I don't care what we have, Natalie. So long as you're both safe, healthy, and part of my world, I'll be happy."

She hugged him tight, kissing him hard. "Good answer."

****

"Did you completely empty the pool?" Natalie asked, moving toward the edge of the large indoor swimming pool.

With Daniel home for the entire month, she had warned him she couldn't shop every single one of those days. So rather than waste their time away, they did things together. The apartment block that he lived at not only had a pool, but also an in-house cinema, a game room, a club, and of course a gym. She hadn't opted for the gym yet.

The thought of watching Daniel work out though actually piqued her interest.

"I didn't make everyone leave. It was already clear when I got here. You took forever." He swam toward the side of the pool, his hands moving to her legs. He spread her legs open, and using the ledge, he lifted up and kissed her.

She sighed.

She was growing addicted to his lips. "You always know what to do to make me want you."

"Come in, the water feels great."

He moved away a little, and she climbed into the pool. The moment she did, he was on her, pressing her against the side of the pool.

Wrapping her legs around him, she moaned as his cock pressed against her core. The bathing suit she wore wasn't enough protection between them. Not that she wanted protection of any sort.

In the past couple of days since Daniel had announced his father's instruction, she had found herself loving the moments she shared with Daniel, his naked body against hers, not to mention the way he took her.

Fucking was all new to her, but with Daniel, she was willing to explore everything.

She ran her tongue across his lips, and he opened up. Their tongues touched, gliding together.

"Now, now. No funny business in the pool,"

Vincent said, entering the room.

What she'd also come to realize was that Ronnie and Vincent were Daniel's personal bodyguards, and where he went, they went.

At night time though, she got him all to herself, with no interference until after they shared breakfast in the morning.

Daniel groaned. "You're taking this protection detail a little too seriously."

"Speak for yourself," Vincent said.

"We're to keep you alive, being the king and all," Ronnie said, dropping into one of the chairs. He wore a pair of swim trunks and sunglasses, even though they were indoors.

"I'm here with my wife."

"We know. Your father wants to make sure that you're always with her, by the way," Vincent said, sitting at the edge of the pool.

"He does?"

"Yep. We got the call. He wants this deal to go off without a hitch."

And like that, any fire that had started died. "Your dad is a cock-block," she said, pulling away from him.

Vincent and Ronnie laughed, and she winked at Daniel.

"You always seem to amaze me."

She tapped her head. "You've not heard everything yet."

"Why do I have a feeling a lifetime with you wouldn't be enough?"

Now that filled her with warmth. He often made comments about them being together for a lifetime. She sometimes wondered if he wanted something similar to her. Love, a future, a chance at a family.

She wanted that.

They may not have started out right, but their life together didn't have to be dictated to by others. They could find a life for themselves.

"Are you being romantic?" Vincent asked.

"Fuck off. This is supposed to be my honeymoon, and I've got two brother-friends ruining it."

"Oh, come on, Natalie likes us, don't you?"

She chuckled. "You're okay. I wouldn't want my man to be upset though."

Daniel moved toward her, and the glint in his eyes sent warmth spreading throughout her entire body.

"Leave," he said.

His voice, the way he spoke, his two friends didn't even bother to argue. They simply grabbed their stuff and began to leave.

"That was a little mean, sending them away."

"They'd have done the same to me if they had what I do."

He moved her so that her back was pressed against the side of the pool.

"Anyone could come in."

"They'll be guarding the doors. No one will come in." His lips slammed down on hers. One of his hands slid in her hair, cupping the back of her head, holding her in place. She couldn't fight, nor did she want to.

His other hand took the strap of her bathing suit and began to slide it down her arm. When it fell loosely, he removed the fabric and cupped her breast. The moment he touched her, she was like fire in his arms.

Wrapping her arms around his neck, she held onto him. He pressed the hard ridge of his cock against her stomach, and together they both moaned.

"You drive me crazy. No one has ever done this to me before."

She didn't want anyone to do this to him ever.

When it came to Daniel, she felt this overwhelming obsession.

He belonged to her, just like she was his.

Running her hands down his body, she found his cock and held him. She remembered everything he'd taught her, how he liked it to be just a little tight. She made sure to give him what he wanted, and as she touched him, he got bigger.

He broke the kiss, trailing his lips down her neck until he took her nipple into his mouth. She closed her eyes, enjoying his touch. Watching his lips circle her tit, she gasped.

Daniel bit down, and the sharp nip took her breath away. He soothed it with his tongue, flicking the tip back and forth.

He teased the other strap of her suit down and removed the fabric, which fell to her waist. He cupped both of her tits, pressing them together, and she couldn't keep touching him as he began to lave her nipples, paying careful attention to each. The fire was more than she could stand.

Pressing her thighs together, she moaned his name, not wanting him to stop.

Daniel released her tits, and her suit was pulled off her body. He placed it on the surface behind her.

His trunks followed suit.

She didn't let him go, and as he pulled her closer, she wrapped her legs around his waist.

One of his hands reached between them, and there in the pool, he teased her, stroking her clit, sliding down, sinking a finger into her pussy. She gasped, moaning his name as he began to fuck her with his finger.

It wasn't enough, though.

He removed his finger, and the tip of his cock began to ease inside her once again. The first initial thrust always shocked her with how big he was. His length drove in, slamming to the hilt and making her cry his name. She didn't want him to stop. He held onto her ass, gripping her tightly as he began to fuck her, going deep with each thrust.

Over and over, he fucked her harder than ever before. It wasn't possible, but it felt like it. Each time they fucked it was the most incredible feeling in the world.

"Please," she said.

"You want to come on my cock, baby?"

"Yes."

"Touch yourself."

She opened her eyes, which had closed the moment he began to touch her. He wouldn't let her go so easily, and she moved her hand between them, finding herself.

With him watching, she started to tease. He began to thrust into her at the same time. Each thrust was shallow at first, then building. She moaned as the sensation took her orgasm to the next level.

It didn't take her long to find her release, and when she did, Daniel filled her with a hard thrust, giving her several seconds to ride her wave of pleasure. The moment she began to come down, his grip on her hips tightened, and he began to fuck her harder, taking her deeper.

He claimed her lips, and she held onto him, relishing the feel of his rock-hard cock driving within her.

"Please, please," she said.

"You've got the best fucking pussy, baby. All I can think about is being inside you."

Over and over, he slammed within her, forcing her need for him even higher.

He didn't let go, and when he found his release, she was desperate for more. The pleasure inside her was not sated as his orgasm spilled inside her.

They were both panting.

Daniel held her close, his kisses adding more fuel to her flame. "I can feel you, Natalie. You want more, don't you?"

"Yes."

"You want me to fuck you again?"

"Yes."

"Good. I'm not done with you yet."

He pulled out of her and helped her climb out of the pool. If she didn't have Daniel's help, she wouldn't have been able to get dressed or focus on anything else. Her body shook with need.

Need for him.

Once they were both dressed, they left the pool. She held Daniel's hand, and pressed her head against his shoulder, not wanting to look at his friends, knowing deep down that they knew what they were doing.

"You can't come upstairs," Daniel said.

"Seriously? Dude, you're putting us to shame."

"Don't care."

They entered the elevator, and she chanced a peek over his shoulder. She didn't know what she expected, but it wasn't to see both friends smiling at him.

They shook their heads but didn't say another word.

"You've got good friends."

"They're the best." He pressed her against the elevator.

"Can't you wait?"

"I'm only going to kiss you." He took possession

of her lips, and she didn't care. Waiting was way overrated.

Chapter Eight

"What?" Daniel asked, pausing as he stared at his father.

He'd been married now for nearly three weeks, and that time had been the best of his life. He couldn't recall a time when he'd been happier.

Staring at his father, he couldn't believe what he was just hearing. This morning had begun with so much promise. Waking up with Natalie in his arms was the pleasure that he didn't think for a second he would have ever found, and yet he had, from their kiss, to their fuck session, where she actually took him in her mouth this morning. He'd guided her through the whole thing, and she'd taken him to the back of her throat, moaning as she did. When he'd been close to orgasm, she'd not left him to it. She kept on sucking his cock until she swallowed down his cum, every last drop.

Daniel had returned the favor, licking her pussy until she screamed his name. Spending time with her was exactly how he imagined it would be. It was the very reason he picked her. But, staring at his father, he couldn't think right now.

"You heard me."

Ronnie and Vincent remained silent as he snorted.

"You're telling me that someone has ordered a hit on my wife," Daniel said. "You don't know who did it?"

He stared at his father. Frank Solano was a tough man, and you didn't argue with him.

"That's what I said." Frank stood up. "You will protect her."

"I want to know what's being done about finding out the perp who fucking did this." Daniel stared at his father. He wasn't leaving until he knew for a fact they were looking into the fucker.

"We're looking."

"You know, I hate to be a party pooper, but it has to be someone on the Valentis' side," Vincent said.

"Why do you figure?" Frank asked. "It could be anyone."

"Not really. Until Daniel married her, Natalie was a no one. She didn't join in the family circles or the social ones. For a long time, Natalie Valenti was just a name. No one knew who she was, or what she did. She was a mystery," Vincent explained, looking mildly bored.

"She's not now," Daniel said.

"I don't see anyone trying to put a hit on our side of things," Ronnie said. "One, it's too dangerous, and two, who would be stupid enough to go up against Daniel?"

Daniel stared at his father. "It has to be Valenti's wife."

"That's a pretty big fucking leap," Frank said. "That is close to an insult, and we don't take kindly to insults."

"I'm not trying to insult anyone. I'm speaking the truth." Daniel stared at his father. For all of the man's faults, he didn't try to have any of them killed. "Natalie's mother tried to kill her twice that we're aware of. It was why she was so close to the cook."

"It's why the dad is close with Natalie," Vincent said. "He had to be in order to keep her safe."

Frank stared at all of them. "You do realize accusing the wife of Valenti could mean certain death. Their reputation alone would see they retaliate."

"We don't ask," Daniel said. "This is my wife. We've heard the news that she's on the hit list. I'm not going to rest until I find this person. In the meantime, we've been invited for family dinner next Sunday."

Frank sighed. "I was hoping not to have to go to that." Daniel watched as his father rubbed his eyes. "You're aware that if the perp is her mother, you will have to demand blood?"

"I will demand her fucking head," Daniel said.

His father looked at him, really looked at him. "This girl has your heart?"

He didn't look away. "I'm in love with my wife, yes."

"That's a pretty big leap in a matter of weeks."

"You don't know her. You've not been around her."

"And you think that would make a difference?"

"It did to me." Daniel didn't back down.

"Loving someone makes you weak."

"Point me in the direction of the fucker who targeted my wife, and you can see how weak I am. Loving Natalie doesn't make me weak. It makes me better, because I will fight harder than anyone else to make it home at night."

Frank kept on staring at him. "If that's what you believe." He moved back behind his desk. "Vincent, Ronnie, leave."

He looked back at his two half-brothers and watched them leave the room. He saw they clearly didn't want to go, yet they did.

Turning his attention back to his father, he waited.

"Is she pregnant?" Frank asked.

"I don't know. It has only been three weeks."

"If the person who hired the hit is her mother, I will take care of it," Frank said. His father sat back in his chair. "You know, this life … it's fucking cruel at times. The money, the power, it doesn't mean shit if you're miserable."

Daniel took a seat as his father began to talk. It was the first time he'd ever spoken to him like this.

"You ever loved anyone?" he asked.

Frank nodded his head. "A long time ago. After you three were born. She worked in a bakery. I pulled over one day after dealing with a rat. I was starving, it was late, and she served me. I don't know why, but I kept on going to that damn bakery for another month. I had on my wedding band, and she wouldn't let anything happen between us. It didn't matter though. I loved the food she had, and the conversation. I'd been with your mother for some time. I couldn't stand her. Most of the women in this life put up with their men. Our marriages are not based on love, but on power. For an entire year, I had her. Piper, her name was. Such a beautiful woman. Sweet smile. She knew who I was, but told me she didn't want to know any of it. I was more than welcome to come, eat my sandwich, and talk." Frank ran a hand down his face. "Love for her made me fucking blind. One of our enemies discovered where I went. He watched me, and because she wasn't a wife, or a daughter, they took her, raped her repeatedly, tortured her, and made her pray for death long before she got it."

Daniel was sure he saw a tear in his father's eye.

"I … she didn't deserve that. I had the tape delivered on the day that I was going to go and see her. I sat and watched what they did to her. They kept her for three days, and I didn't even know they had her."

"What did you do?"

"I set fire to this fucking city. I made sure I found every single person that helped. I killed everyone—and they did it because I liked her. She was a no one, just someone special to me. It was the only time I actually considered a life far away from this one. A white picket fence, three-bedroom home, a dog maybe. Loving someone can make you weak to others seeing what you love. I don't have a problem with you loving Natalie, son. In fact, I'd say that I was happy for you. I know I don't show it, but you'll understand one day. You've got to keep your shit together, as otherwise someone will exploit what you love. Keep her close, and keep your eye on the ball."

Daniel nodded.

His father waved his hand, letting him know he was dismissed.

Vincent and Ronnie were waiting for him, along with Natalie. When he got the call demanding all of their presences, he didn't have much choice but to bring her to his childhood home. She'd opted to sit outside his office. There were a couple of guards he was sure she talked to. His mother didn't even bother to come and see her.

"All set?" she asked.

"All set."

"So, I booked us a place at this Italian restaurant. Theodore told me all about this place, and they have the best carbonara going, and I love carbonara. Do you like Italian?"

He smiled. "I do." As he wrapped his arm around her shoulders, they left the house. "Do you talk to everyone?"

"Only the people that I like."

Her arm held him close, and not for the first time, he wondered if she liked him the way he liked her.

No, not liked, *loved*.

Watching her sleep, he'd known that he'd fallen in love with her. He had to wonder, though, if her feelings were the same. He'd taken her away from the life she'd originally had planned. Was there even a smidgen of a chance that she could love him?

****

Later that night, Natalie sat in bed waiting for Daniel to arrive. When he'd left his father's office earlier before she made them all go to dinner, she'd seen the tension. Ronnie and Vincent had tried to hide what was going on with their jokes and laughter. She didn't get it.

Running fingers through her hair, she couldn't wait for him to come to bed. He'd been in the shower for a long time. Climbing out of bed, she made her way toward the kitchen and made herself a hot chocolate.

With her mug full, she moved toward the windows and opened up one of the curtains. The city below was aglow with activity. She sipped at her chocolate and thought about the life that she was currently living. It seemed surreal to her that she was married to Daniel Solano, and she was happy.

Her happiness was the most confusing part about it all. She hadn't expected to be happy or joyous; far from it. Taking another long sip, she saw her reflection in the mirror. She wore a sexy negligee. The only reason she wore them was so Daniel had a reason to take them off. She loved his rough hands as they tugged the fabric from her. Not only did she love his hands, but his sexy words. The way he commanded her.

She loved everything about him, and that was what made her life so much more enjoyable.

In the past few weeks, she'd seen something inside him, and it had taken her feelings for him to the next level.

Love wasn't allowed in their world.

A world she'd tried desperately to leave behind.

"Why are you out here?" Daniel said, catching her unaware. She gasped, and nearly spilled her hot chocolate.

She saw there was no spillage and smiled at him.

"Nearly."

He wrapped an arm around her waist, closed the curtain, and pulled her back into the room.

"Okay, you see, there's only so much of this silent, brooding treatment I'm willing to take. It's getting a little … boring."

She turned in his arm, and his hand rested on her hip. She tried not to think of all the dirty things he could do to her body. Right now, she needed to focus on what was going on with him, and he couldn't lie. She saw the trouble in his eyes, and she had a right to know the truth.

"Tell me," she said. "Since you met your father, something has been bugging you, and I can't handle it. We're a team, Daniel."

He took her hand within both of his, pressing a kiss to her knuckles.

"Don't you dare say you're handling it," she said.

Daniel smirked. "I *am* handling it."

"Oh, how do you expect this to work if you keep me in the dark? I don't know what you want from me."

"Someone has put a hit out on you."

Her mouth opened, then closed, and opened again.

"A hit on me?"

"Yes. Someone wants you dead."

"Oh." She licked her lips and stood back. Staring at her empty hot chocolate mug, she needed to go and clean it up. Brushing past him, she made her way toward the sink, and began to wash the dirty cup.

Daniel didn't leave her alone for long. He moved right up behind her, wrapping his arms around her waist. His hands rested on her stomach.

When he pulled her back, there was no evidence of his arousal.

"The thought of my death doesn't get you off?"

she asked.

"Don't, Natalie. Please."

"So, someone has ordered a hit on me." She finished cleaning the cup and reached for the towel. All the time, Daniel kept a hold of her waist, not letting her go.

She didn't want his arms to be anywhere else but around her.

"Yes."

She released a breath. "Wow."

"I think it's your mother."

"Oh." Now that didn't actually surprise her. Her mother had been wanting her dead for a long time. "Your father knew?"

"He knew, and he warned me."

"Do you want me to get Dad on the phone?" she asked.

"It's not something you can just make a phone call about, baby. I accuse his wife, and it's not true, he'd have to retaliate."

"Even though we're married?" She didn't like this.

"Yes. It's just the way they work."

"I don't want anything to happen to you."

"I won't let anything happen to me, either. I love coming home to you too much to set you free."

This made her smile. When he used the word *love*, it made her believe in fantasies. Could he love her one day?

Turning in his arms, she stared into his eyes. "How?"

"How what?"

"How can you find out if it's my mom? Dad would never tell you."

"We'll find a way."

"What happens?" she asked.

"She put a hit out on my wife. You're not a Valenti anymore. She's willing to try to kill what was mine, and I would have to put a stop to it. Blood would have to be spilled."

"I don't know why she hates me so much," she said.

"You think it's your mother?"

"She's the only one that has already tried to kill me, so yeah, I would say she's the one who wants me dead."

He held her tightly to him, his hands running up and down her back.

She closed her eyes. Even though the topic they were talking about was the least erotic, her body began to wake with his touch.

Her pussy grew slick, and her nipples tightened.

Against her stomach, she felt his cock begin to thicken, and she bit her lip, trying to contain her smile.

His hands moved down to her ass, squeezing the flesh. She released a little moan.

In one swift move, he lifted her up and placed her on the counter.

Running her hands down his body, she took his kiss the moment his lips were on hers. Cupping his face, she gasped as he spread her legs open. He stepped between them, lifting up her negligee, exposing her pussy.

Within seconds, he had his cock in his hand and eased the tip up and down her wet slit. She cried out his name as he slid inside her. Each inch filling her made her ache for more.

He tore at the straps of her negligee, which fell to her waist. He cupped her tits, lifting them up. His tongue teased across each nipple as he pressed them together.

Gripping the counter, she couldn't contain her moans as he rocked within her, going deeper with each thrust.

"I will protect you, Natalie. You're mine, and I wouldn't let anything happen to you. I will always keep you safe."

"I believe you."

He lifted her off the counter, still with his dick inside her. She gasped, wrapping her arms around him as he carried her back through to their bedroom. He followed her down to the bed, his cock slamming inside her.

They moved and fucked their way until they were against the pillows. Daniel took her hands, pressing them either side of her head. He held her down and began to drive his cock within her.

"Watch us, baby. Watch as I fuck you."

She looked down, seeing his cock appear before sliding deeper within her. She couldn't contain her moan, the pleasure of his touch driving her arousal higher. She needed him more than anything.

"Fuck, baby, I want you so much."

Over and over, he drove within her, taking her to the next level. He released her hands and sat back. His fingers found her clit, teasing her pussy, drawing an orgasm from her.

Before she'd come down from her peak, he filled her again, rocking inside her, harder than ever before.

She loved the power of his possession, the ache that flooded her. Daniel was everything she ever wanted, and as he came, flooding her pussy with his cum, she wished he loved her.

To make her life perfect, she craved his love.

He collapsed against her, and she held him tightly.

She closed her eyes, pushing away the tears that

sprang to her eyes thinking about all that he'd told her. The saddest thing of all, she wasn't even surprised, not even a little bit. Her mother had no love for her. Other than Mary and her father, there was no one else that loved her.

This was why she tried to avoid thinking about her family.

She hated feeling this way, and it was one of the reasons she'd tried to leave.

Daniel pulled away from her, and she forced a smile to her lips. He tensed up. "What is it?" he asked.

"It's nothing. I'm fine."

"You look like I've hurt you. I didn't hurt you."

He pulled out of her, and began to look her over, searching for bruises or something like that.

"It's nothing, honestly, that was perfect."

"If it was perfect, you wouldn't be close to tears."

She cupped his face and smiled. "Thank you."

He took her hand, kissing her knuckles. "What?"

"Just being silly."

"I will do everything I can to protect you, Natalie. I can only do that if you're honest with me."

"I'm not surprised by what you've said. I'm just, it still hurts, you know?"

"She's not worth this. You're better than her, but don't ever hold back. I want you to be honest with me. Promise."

"I promise."

Chapter Nine

Daniel hadn't wanted to come to Sunday lunch with the Valenti family. Any reason from Natalie and he'd have been more than willing to cancel. His father hadn't told him if her mother was the person behind the hired hit.

He stood in the sitting room, watching as Louisa and her mother stood talking to each other. Everyone looked normal. Alfie was talking with Frank. Vincent and Ronnie were with him, as he wouldn't go anywhere without them.

Natalie's brothers were sitting there, drinking.

Seconds passed, and Natalie finally appeared. She carried a tray of drinks, these non-alcoholic.

She came toward him, placing a drink in his hand first. The scent of coffee soothed his senses, but he looked at his wife, who looked stressed.

"You okay?" he asked, taking her hand, and placing a kiss to her knuckles.

"I'm fine. Just a little … tense."

"Go and get your own drinks." He told Vincent and Ronnie before taking Natalie into his arms. Her ass rested against his cock.

She gave him a little wriggle, and he leaned forward, grazing her ear. "You're playing with fire."

"I like to play. Would you play with me?" she asked. Her head rested against his chest, and she smiled up at him. His cock twitched just thinking about all the kinds of play they could have.

"You look like the happy couple," Louisa said, speaking up from her position.

No one saw it, but he felt Natalie's tension.

"That's because we're very happy," he said, speaking up. He looked around the room. Each person had a reason to try to kill Natalie. The only one who ever *had* tried was the woman glaring at her though.

She was the easiest target to attack. Louisa, though, she loved money, and a lifestyle. She may take soldiers as lovers, but they'd never have the kind of power he or anyone like him would. Word would have gotten around that he'd passed her ass up, and it would make other men think twice about being with her.

Then of course, there were Natalie's brothers. They were thirsty for blood, and a peace between Valenti and Solano would end any chance of war. Could they decide to take out his wife in order to incite it?

It couldn't be her father. He wanted peace.

No, he had money on the mother, the sister, or the brothers. He held onto her hip, stroking her, letting her knew with his touch alone that he was there for her. That she didn't have to be afraid.

"You're happy?" Alfie asked, looking at his daughter.

Natalie nodded. "Yes, very happy. Daniel takes care of everything."

"She also has two best friends, slash brothers, with her at all times," Daniel said, nodding at Vincent and Ronnie. "I like to make sure she's protected." He was purposefully making comments just to see who would bite, and who would not.

His father was aware of what he was doing.

"It's been a pleasure, Alfie, to finally bring peace to our families. Natalie is a treasure. You must all be proud of her," Frank said.

Her mother sneered, and Louisa looked disgusted.

"It took us by surprise. You wanting the fat sister," her brother said.

Natalie didn't even gasp or make a move at her brother's words.

"That is my daughter-in-law," Frank said, being the first to speak up. "Seeing as we're all family right now, I suggest you apologize."

"She's my sister. I can say what I want to."

"Not in front of me, you cannot. I will demand respect," Frank said. His gaze landed on Alfie. "Now."

Alfie demanded his son apologize.

Silence fell for the longest time before he finally did. Daniel didn't like it. He didn't like any of this.

"Alfie, I'd like to talk to you privately," Daniel said. He wanted Alfie to be aware of what was going on.

Part of him wondered if the whole family had a hit on her.

When Natalie went to leave, he wouldn't let her. Vincent and Ronnie nodded at him, and they stepped out. They were his eyes and ears. Only his father, Alfie, Natalie, and himself remained.

"Natalie, I'm sorry—"

"I'm not here about that," Daniel said.

"A hit has been placed on Natalie," Frank said.

Alfie went pale. Daniel wouldn't let his woman go. She wasn't going to go and comfort the older man. As far as he was concerned, Alfie hadn't done enough to protect her. Alfie should have killed his wife long ago for what she'd been willing to do to a baby.

"What? That's not possible," Alfie said. "Natalie has never really been part—"

"It's one of the four people who has just left," Daniel said. "Her mother, sister, or brothers."

Alfie cursed and walked away. "They have no reason to go after her."

"They don't? What about our marriage? Louisa has no other prospects for a good husband. Your wife has already tried to kill her. Your sons want to make a name for themselves. They want to start a war, and targeting my wife will get them that."

Natalie held his arm, and he felt her shaking a little bit. It was one thing to be told this when you were far away from the people who could want you dead. Right now, she was in the sitting room, and a few minutes ago, she'd been near the people who could very well want her dead.

"I won't protect them," Alfie said, looking at them. "Whoever ordered it, you do what you need to do. I won't help them murder my daughter. You have my permission to take blood."

That was all they needed.

"Why does blood have to be spilled?" Natalie asked.

"It's our way. If your mother really has done this, I don't see any other way," Alfie said.

The pain on his face was clearly visible, which told Daniel one thing: he really believed it was her mother.

Alfie took Natalie's hands, pulling her closer. He cupped her face, and the love there, it was real for all to see. "Are you really happy?"

"I told you I was. I'm really happy."

"Good. I know you didn't want this."

She chuckled. "Living with Daniel isn't bad. He's also got two awesome friends as well. I'm happy, really happy."

Daniel smiled, and nodded at Alfie.

"Can I talk to Alfie alone for a minute?" Daniel asked.

"Come, Natalie," Frank said. "I'll keep you safe from the wicked witch."

He loved hearing her laughter, and knew he was going to spend the rest of his life just waiting to hear that sound.

"What would you like to talk to me about?" Alfie asked the moment the door closed.

"I'd never hurt Natalie, sir." Daniel paid him the respect he believed he was due. It was the least he could do after everything.

"You compliment me, but I don't deserve it." Alfie moved to pour himself a scotch. Daniel watched him. "You see, any other sane man would have put a bullet in his wife years ago. Especially when he realized she was capable of killing their child."

"Why didn't you?"

"I'm sentimental. No, that's bullshit. I couldn't. My wife comes from a strong family. Killing her would have caused an all-out war, and I didn't have the resources. It wasn't safe for anyone for me to kill her. I should have, and consequences be damned, but I couldn't. My hands were tied." Alfie shrugged. "We never got on. We forced everything. I couldn't stand her. She didn't want me. Our families needed to marry, and I had no choice but to take her. She didn't want my kids. I didn't want her touch. After giving birth to two sons and a daughter, that was it. Then in one night of madness, we fucked and ended up with Natalie. I think she resented that. She hated that she proved to be weak." Alfie shrugged. "Oh, well, not a lot I can do. I just … out of all of my kids, Natalie was always so sweet, so special, so smart, and I wanted the best for her. I still do. She made me smile even when I had to make decisions that I didn't like."

"I love her," Daniel said.

"Does she know?"

"Not yet. I don't think she's ready to hear that, but when she is, I'll tell her."

Alfie nodded. "That's good. She deserves someone who will love her unconditionally. That's all she really wanted. Not to be forced into a marriage like this. You're a good man, Daniel. You'll get things right where your father and I failed. Let's go and eat dinner."

****

Natalie sat beside Daniel, and it had to be one of the tensest dinners she'd ever had the displeasure of sitting at. Alfie and Frank kept up the conversation. Her brothers didn't look impressed, and her sister kept making love eyes to a different guard this time.

Underneath the table, Daniel had caught her hand and given it a squeeze, and his attempt to comfort her filled her with warmth.

Pushing her food around the plate, she wondered what life would have been like if Louisa had married him. Just the thought of it sent pain shooting through her heart.

Daniel was hers.

He'd picked *her*.

Once they got to the dessert, she was ready to go home. Vincent and Ronnie were their usual teasing selves, and she couldn't help but laugh at them.

"Excuse me," Frank said, putting his cell phone to his ear and leaving the table. Alfie went a little pale, and Daniel's frown got firmer.

Most awkward dinner on the planet.

"So, you're both happily married?" Louisa asked. "No fighting? No cross words?"

"We don't argue," Daniel said.

"Please, that's got to be impossible. Natalie never wanted to marry into this life. She didn't want to be a killer's wife."

Natalie stared at her sister. "I'm happy to be with Daniel." She offered him a smile. "We're working through everything."

"Besides, she gets to hang with us," Ronnie said,

taking a piece of bread and chewing it with his mouth open. She knew he was doing it on purpose to annoy people. She found it rather funny.

"I don't think it's right that you're alone with other men. Your husband needs to know that he can trust you," her mother said, finally speaking up. The hard edge of her tone wasn't lost on anyone.

"You have nothing to worry about. I know my wife wouldn't stray." Daniel released her hand and stroked her hair.

She turned toward him, turning to kiss his palm. "No, I wouldn't. I have no need to." She closed her eyes as his fingers teased her neck. She didn't want to stray, and there was no one else in her life nor any temptation to do so. Everything her heart had ever wanted was right here, for all to see.

If only he loved her.

She didn't know if he was even capable of loving her. She hoped he was.

Love was something she'd wanted more than anything of.

Frank came in, clearing his voice and pocketing his cell phone.

Natalie turned toward him and gasped. He had a gun pointed at her mother's head.

"What is the meaning of this?" Louisa said.

"Leave this room now!" Frank bellowed out the order, and Alfie stood. "I have confirmation that she ordered the rape and murder of my daughter-in-law. You wanted him to hurt her. To take everything away from her, and to make it hurt."

"I did no such thing," she said.

Natalie wasn't surprised.

No one moved as Frank grabbed the back of her head and pressed it against the table. "I've spoken to the man you hired. You see, whore, I have contacts everywhere. The moment you ordered that hit, I was aware of it. I was just trying to find the person who was behind the hit. He was more than willing to use you as a shield. He's paid to do a job, and now I'm paying him to stand down."

Daniel pulled Natalie to her feet, and she was suddenly standing behind him.

Her mother began to laugh. "I should have killed that bitch years ago, but everyone stopped me. Every time I look at her, I remember that I gave in. That I fucking caved. She had no right to be here, and you," her gaze landed on Alfie, "you loved her the most. Just making my life even more miserable. You loved her to spite me."

Tears filled her eyes.

"Yes, I ordered her death. I wanted her gone so I didn't have to look at her again. She's a fucking whore. A waste of space and should have never been born."

"That's my wife," Daniel said. "You would have taken her from the Solanos. The debt must be repaid."

A single shot was fired, and Natalie held onto Daniel, scared. Frank hadn't fired his gun. She turned to see her father's weapon drawn.

He'd shot his wife.

Frank released her, and her body slumped to the ground.

Her brothers and Louisa hadn't had time to react or to leave.

"Mark my words, if any of you step out of line again, you will be like she is," Alfie said. "I need a fucking drink." She glanced at her father, and he gave them a nod. "I think dinner is finished for today."

No one else spoke as he left the room.

Daniel took charge, leading her out of the house

and placing her in the back of the car. Vincent was with her, and Ronnie stayed with him.

"Come with me. Don't stay here."

"I've got to stay here." He gripped the back of her neck, pulling her close. "I'll see you tonight."

She watched him leave, and she ached for him.

"I'm so sorry you had to see that," Vincent said.

"My mother absolutely hated me."

"Because you reminded her that she was human, and could have feelings. Don't let this concern you."

The drive back to Daniel's penthouse apartment was a blur. She didn't see much of what happened.

Her mother had ordered to have her raped and killed.

It was kind of … surreal.

Entering the apartment, she left Vincent alone and took a shower, a really long one that didn't help to clear her thoughts any.

Dressed in a white robe, she lay down on their bed, hers and Daniel's, and stared at nothing.

Hearing her mother's spite once again, it was nothing different from all the years she'd heard it before. The anger, the rage—at least now she understood it. Her mother had prided herself on not responding to Alfie, on hating him, and Natalie's very presence had showed that at least one night, that wasn't the case. One night she'd given in to lust, and probably really enjoyed it.

Time passed, and the bed dipped. Daniel appeared. Tears were running across her face, dripping onto the bed.

He was fully clothed. He covered her hands with his. "Hey, baby," he said.

"Hey."

"I didn't want to leave you."

"I know. You didn't really have much choice

though, did you? Busy life, duty calls and all that."

He smiled, pressing a kiss to her hands. He reached out, stroking some of her hair back behind her ear.

"She's gone."

"Yep, she's gone. The debt is paid, and no one is ever going to hurt you again."

"She hated me, Daniel. She hated me so much that she paid someone to come and kill me."

"I'll never let anything happen to you. Not now, not ever. I promise you that."

She nodded and moved toward him. Resting her head on his chest, she closed her eyes. "I'd really like that."

"Can I ask you something?"

"Yes. You can ask me anything, Daniel."

His arms surrounded her, and the chill she'd been feeling since her mother's hatred was once again spilled, was finally receding. "Are you really happy with me?"

She tilted her head back to look at him and smiled. "Yes, I am. Is that hard to believe?"

"I know you didn't want this life."

"I didn't, but I think I got really lucky because you're one in a billion, Daniel." She cupped his cheek. "Yes, I'm happy. Are you happy with me?"

"I couldn't wish or want another wife."

His hand splayed across her back, and she rested her head against his shoulder. Love would come, she had to believe that. She would never give up trying.

Chapter Ten

A couple months later

"Have you told her yet?" Vincent asked.

Daniel stared at his friends. They were in one of the Solano nightclubs. It had been a busy time for them at work. His father was slowly passing more and more work to him, which he didn't mind. He was a Solano, and he knew there was no way out for him.

"Told who what?" Vincent's date asked. She was a perky little blonde. Not much going on upstairs, but totally Vincent's type.

At Natalie's request, she asked Ronnie and Vincent to have dates so that it didn't feel like they were all on assignment watching them. She didn't like having bodyguards. Not that he'd consider his two best friends just bodyguards. They were the only two men in the world he'd ever trust with her safety. No doubt about it.

"Our boy here is in love and has been for some time."

"That's really nice." The girl pressed her hands together. "Love is so romantic."

Ronnie came back with his own girl hanging around his neck.

"Natalie went to the bathroom."

Finishing off his drink, Daniel made his way toward the private bathrooms. She'd been on the dance floor with Ronnie's girlfriend as he had to take a call at the time.

Entering the bathroom, he heard someone vomiting. Going past three stalls, he came to the fourth and saw Natalie throwing up.

Moving into the toilet, he wrapped her hair around his fist, keeping it back. The long locks felt soft against his hand, and his dick protested. If she was vomiting like this, he wasn't going to get any fun tonight.

Running his hand down her back, he waited patiently as she kept throwing everything up.

"My body hates me."

"Was it something you ate?" he asked. They had all eaten the same thing.

"No, I don't think this is something I ate."

She stood up, flushing the toilet.

Releasing her hair, he watched as she leaned over the sink, and began to press water against her face and neck.

"What do you think it is?"

Natalie stared at his reflection, and reached into her bag, pulling out a packet of something. "I bought this today," she said. "I was looking into morning sickness, and did you know it doesn't always have to stay during the morning? It could happen any time."

She held a pregnancy test kit.

He didn't wear a rubber when he was with her, and he didn't want one now. "Do you know if you are or not?"

"I've not … I didn't want to take it without you. I was going to tell you tonight after we had some fun. I wanted you to be with me when this happened. Is that crazy?"

He stepped up close. "Not crazy at all."

"Please don't kiss me. I have vomit breath." She even put her hand up to cover her mouth when she did it.

"Do you want to wait until we get home? Have some fun?" He'd wait if she wanted it.

"It would be kind of hard. If I'm pregnant I don't want to risk having anything bad to drink." She stared at the box. "Would it really hurt finding out in a nightclub?"

"I don't think it would hurt at all. I don't mind

how we find out so long as we know the truth."

"That's what I was thinking."

She opened up the box and handed him the instructions. He read through them. His stomach was fucking flipping.

They could be pregnant. Staring at her stomach, he thought about her swollen with his kid, and all he wanted to do was fuck her, to take her hard and fuck her until she couldn't think of anyone else.

"I'll … go and pee."

She entered the cubicle, and when someone entered the bathroom, he ordered them to fuck off.

He didn't hear any sound of her peeing. "You okay in there?"

"Right now, I don't think I can do this."

"We can go home? I can tickle you."

This brought a chuckle from her. "You're crazy, you know that, right?"

"Yep." *It's why you love me.*

She hadn't said the words, and he didn't expect her to.

He heard her finally releasing, and when it was done, she came out. Her cheeks were bright red. "I don't even want to talk about what just happened."

This only made him laugh harder.

She washed her hands and placed the stick on the counter. He was already checking his watch to see how long they had to wait.

They both leaned against the sink, waiting.

"Do you want kids?"

"Yeah, I want kids. I can see you, pregnant, and I wonder if I'll get to feel our son or daughter kick." He took her hand. "Do you want this?"

"I'd love to be a mom. Just … yes, I want to be a mom. I hope I'm better than my own."

"You don't want to hurt our baby, so I'd say you're already better than her."

She smiled. "I hope so. God, what if I'm not pregnant?"

"Then you ate something and we take you to a doctor to get you fixed."

"You always think of everything."

"And you always panic about everything. You don't need to panic about any of this. I've got you. I will always have you, Natalie." He glanced down at his watch, and the time was up. "It's ready."

"Wow, I'm so nervous." She breathed out a sigh. "Are you ready?"

"As I'll ever be."

They both turned and Natalie picked up the stick, and together they saw that it had the two lines.

"I'm pregnant," she said. "We're pregnant."

She turned toward him.

"We're going to have a baby?" he asked.

He pulled her into his arms, holding her close. He went to kiss her, but Natalie pulled away. "I need to brush my teeth."

Daniel didn't kiss her. He wanted to, but he knew she would hate that. Stroking her cheek, he smiled at her.

"What is it?" she asked.

"I am the luckiest guy in the world, do you know that? So fucking lucky."

"I think I got just as lucky. Maybe even more so. You could have totally been an asshole."

"I could still be an asshole," he said. "Damn, woman, I love you."

He spoke the words that he'd been wanting to say to her for a long time, but simply hadn't. With work, and everything that had happened, he'd wanted to tell her at exactly the right time, but the life he led, there never was a right time.

She released a little gasp. "You love me?"

"Yes, and I'm not just saying that about the fact we're going to have kids."

"I'm pregnant with one baby. We don't know if it will be twins."

"I don't care. I know we're going to have lots of them, and we're going to build a family together, and it's going to be amazing because you're amazing. You're the love of my life, Natalie. It's why I couldn't be without you. It's why I never want to be without you. I love you more than anything else in the world."

Tears filled her eyes, and he didn't want to be responsible for making her cry.

"Don't cry," he said.

"They're really happy tears. I'm really happy," she said. "You love me, and I love you too. I've loved you for so long, but I've been so afraid to tell you, and now I can't stop crying."

"It's probably the hormones."

"I didn't want to be part of this crazy life where people killed other people for fun, but I will do anything to be with you. You're the only man I want, and I love you so much."

He pulled her into his arms, holding her close.

"I want to kiss you, but now I hate that I don't have any mints."

"How about, we tell them the good news, then we leave, and you can brush your teeth, and I can kiss you all night long."

"I love the sound of that."

Laughing, he took her hand and led her back out to where his friends were waiting.

"Took you long enough," Vincent said.

"We're pregnant," Daniel said.

Cheers went around the table.

"And we're going to go and leave. Make this a two-people celebration. We'll talk tomorrow."

He didn't give them time to talk. As he pulled Natalie out of the bar, his car was already waiting for him. He helped her inside, placing the seatbelt around her and making sure she was secure.

She giggled. "I'm fine. I'm safe."

"Good."

He would keep her and his child safe.

He'd do everything to make sure he had them both.

****

With her teeth now brushed, Natalie made her way back to the bedroom where Daniel caught her around the waist, spinning her to face him.

His lips were on hers, and she gripped the back of his neck, holding him close. He moved her back until she was pressed against the wall. He took hold of her hands and placed them flat on either side of her head.

"You're feeling kinky tonight?" she asked.

He chuckled. "I want to love every single inch of you."

"I'm all yours, Daniel. Every single part of me belongs to you."

Daniel took possession of her lips, and it wasn't long before he touched her neck, sucking on her pulse. She loved it when he kissed her neck, especially when he had a day's stubble, and it felt so good.

He didn't stop there.

"Keep your hands above your head."

She held her hands where he told her, and he tore the negligee from her body.

He loved her.

This man. The guy she hadn't wanted to marry

loved her.

Her feelings for him hadn't been instant. They had taken time, but the moment she got to know the real man beneath the title, she'd fallen for him hard. The world got to see the bad guy, but she got to see *him*.

His lips moved to her breasts, and as she stared in the mirror she watched as he took one nipple into his mouth. His hand cupped the other, pinching the tip.

"I love your tits. They're going to get bigger as well."

She gasped as he pinched one. He moved toward the one he hadn't sucked, flicking it with his tongue. His touch set her on fire. She wanted more of him, craved him.

Her pussy was already soaking wet.

She wanted him.

Needed him.

Was desperate to feel him fucking her.

Daniel wasn't in a rush though.

He took his time, lavishing each nipple until he was satisfied. There was no rushing him. She knew from experience that he loved to drive her wild, to take her to the peak, and push her over the edge. Of course, right now he kept her at the edge, waiting.

"How is your pussy?"

"Please, Daniel, I can't take much more."

He knelt on the floor, and she opened her legs. This time, he didn't make her wait long as his tongue touched her clit. He stroked over the nub and she gasped, her head resting against the wall. The pleasure was already to the point of pain, burning for more, for everything that he had to give her.

"You taste so good."

Daniel moved her away from the wall, walking her back until her legs hit the bed. He followed her down.

He pressed two fingers inside her, and his tongue danced back and forth over her clit.

Gripping the sheet beneath her, she rocked her pussy up against his face, needing him.

"Please, I can't take much more. I need it. Don't stop. Please."

He didn't stop, and when her orgasm came, she was so fucking ready for it.

Screaming his name, she went over the edge, to the point that stars danced behind her eyes. The pleasure was unlike anything she'd ever felt before, and he kept her there, sending her into a second orgasm.

He didn't wait for her to come down from this peak though.

Daniel spread her legs, and his cock glided between her slick folds. He entered her and slammed every single inch within her.

He took hold of her hands, and he wasn't gentle to start off. Each thrust seared her to the core, not in a bad way. Her pussy was so wet that as he took her roughly, he filled her with ease.

"Fuck, baby, you feel so good. This is my pussy, and I love being inside you." He pressed his lips against hers, and she tasted herself on him, and she didn't care.

This was hard, dirty, and everything she wanted.

He surrounded her. His smell, everything. She was addicted to him, and only him.

There was no way she ever wanted anyone else.

This life hadn't been what she thought she wanted, but she wanted him, and would do everything for him.

Daniel was her life. He was her soul, and she'd do anything to keep him.

Suddenly, Daniel slowed down, his thrusts going from frantic to slow. He teased her with his cock, holding her hands to the bed as he pulled all the way out of her. The tip of his cock slid across her pussy, bumping her clit, making her gasp. He slid back inside her.

"You're so wet, baby."

She felt her wetness leaking from her.

Daniel clearly relished her arousal, and she refused to be embarrassed by what he did to her.

"You want my cock."

"Yes."

He fucked inside her three times, and she cried out, wanting more.

Daniel took her to the peak, keeping her there, and they danced together, him in charge, like always.

She didn't want it to stop, and as he brought her to a third orgasm, she felt it as he found his own release. His cum filled her pussy, flooding her with his seed.

He collapsed over her, taking most of his weight so that he didn't crush her.

She wrapped her arms around his back and smiled at him.

"Do you have any idea what you do to me?" he asked.

"I imagine it's similar to what you do to me. That was incredible."

"I love you," he said.

This just made her smile even more. "And I love you."

He pushed some of her hair off her face, and he moved, still with his dick inside her, but so that he lay on the bed. He rested his head in his hands, and she touched him, resting her hand on his arm.

"Was this how you imagined it would be?" she asked.

"No, I didn't know how it would be." He cupped her cheek. "There is no one else I'd rather spend my life with. I hope you know that."

She nodded. "I know that."

"And I will never stop loving you. You're the only woman I want, Natalie."

"No mistresses then."

He shook his head. "None. No woman will ever match up to you."

All of her life she'd wanted someone who would love her without restraint, who wouldn't care what other people thought or saw. After what her mother put her through, a life filled with vile, nasty comments, she'd thought she could handle anything.

Her mother had nearly broken her, but Daniel was the one who had put her back together.

Taking hold of his hand, she locked her fingers with his. They were bound together not only in marriage and blood, but also in love.

"I'm yours, forever, Daniel. I'll never leave, and I will do everything to make a life with you one that you wish to come home to."

He leaned forward and kissed her.

This time, she felt his love right down to her soul, and knew she'd never give it up, not a chance in the world.

Epilogue

Five years later

"This is our last baby," Daniel said.

Natalie looked up at her husband. "You said that after Charlotte, then of course you said it after Dylan, and now you're saying it again, after Rose."

He smiled down at his wife. Yes, their little girl had nearly given him a heart attack. He stood behind Natalie, one hand pressed against her head, breathing in her scent. He loved his kids. They made him want to be a better man, but his wife?

His love for Natalie was what drove him insane.

Vincent and Ronnie had gotten him a book on pregnancy, and being the kind of guy that he was, he'd read the damn thing. It was all fine. He knew each week, each little stage, and how big their baby was going to be.

He'd been there for the kicking, and the heartburn, and of course the long nights when she couldn't sleep. Every step of the way with each pregnancy he'd been there.

Then of course, there had been the complications section in the book, and with that, he'd gone and done more research.

Now, only a slim number of women didn't survive pregnancy or the birthing stage, but knowing there was a risk, it had driven him crazy with worry.

Natalie had told him everything would be fine, but the thought of living without her, of possibly having to be with a child that he knew had killed his wife, would have destroyed him. He'd even told Ronnie and Vincent that if anything happened to her, they had to end him. His love for her was that fucking strong.

With Charlotte's labor, it had taken a long time, a day, but to him it had lasted weeks. He'd even threatened the doctor that if anything happened to his woman, he'd kill him, and then his family, and then of course, he'd kill him again.

She took his hand and placed it on Rose's chest. Their little girl was wriggling about. She'd screamed as they always do, which was a good sound. The doctors had smiled, and then as she was placed in her mother's arms, Rose had gone quiet.

"Hello, little girl, our little baby daughter. I'm Mommy, and this is Daddy. Don't mind him though. He's a little cranky because you took too long. I know your brother and your sister are going to love you oh, so much, and it's going to be amazing." Natalie kissed her head, and then looked up at him. "Hold her."

She made him do this each and every time.

Kissing her lips, he leaned forward and took his little girl in his arms. All the while, Natalie smiled at him. "She's so perfect," she said.

He stared down at his little girl, with her perfect lips, nose, and her eyes, staring up at him.

There he went. The tightening of his chest. The love that he felt and the protectiveness all came rushing forward for his little baby.

"And that's Daddy, Rose," Natalie said.

She covered his hand with her own.

"Well, maybe we could have one more," he said, seeing the love in her eyes. He couldn't deny her, would never dream of denying her.

Natalie rested her head against his arm and giggled. "I know how to get what I want." She winked at him, and he saw that she was tired.

Rose gave a little whimper, and he placed her back in Natalie's arms. She kept sniffing out her breast, and he watched as Natalie placed Rose against her nipple, and their little girl began to nurse.

"I love you," Natalie said. "More than anything in the world." She leaned against him, and he kissed her head.

"There are no words," he said.

He'd lost the words long ago.

Natalie was his, and she would always belong to him.

The love he had for her didn't have any boundaries.

The End

www.samcrescent.com

HIS TO TAKE

www.ingramcontent.com/pod-product-compliance
Lightning Source LLC
Chambersburg PA
CBHW022036170626
46808CB00003B/1234